D1116767

A Season In-Between

A SEASON

IN-BETWEEN

 Jan Greenberg

Farrar · Straus · Giroux | *New York*

Grateful acknowledgment is made to Melody Trails, Inc.,
for permission to use lyrics for Turn! Turn! Turn!,
adaptation and music by Pete Seeger,
TRO-copyright © 1962 Melody Trails, Inc.

Library of Congress Cataloging in Publication Data
Greenberg, Jan.
A season in-between.
SUMMARY: At a time when her life is consumed by the
exhausting task of growing up, Carrie's stable home life is
drastically altered.
[1. Death—Fiction] I. Title.
PZ7.G8438Se   1979   [Fic]   79–17997
ISBN 0–374–36564–4

---

*For my daughters
Lynne, Jeanne & Jackie
with love*

A Season In-Between

I

I was sitting on the grass in my skunk costume when it occurred to me that my partner, a squirrel otherwise known as Courtney Allen, had disappeared. We were rehearsing for the May Day Festival, an annual event at Miss Elliot's Academy. The rites of spring at a private girls' school are nothing like the bawdy celebration of medieval times, but Courtney was doing her best to revive old customs. I spotted her shaggy, crepe-paper tail sticking out of the bushes. Emerging from the other end was a mop of curly red hair that could only belong to Scott Carouthers, an eighth-grade potential dropout from Woodson Hall Prep. He stalks Courtney with the eager enthusiasm of a good squirrel hunter.

Now don't get frantic, I told myself, but our turn to scamper onto the meadow was fast approaching, and I didn't want to explain Courtney's absence.

Courtney is my sometimes friend, depending on her mood and the availability of her numerous other resources. Usually I cover up for her when she is missing, which happens frequently now that she's discovered boys. Boys have also discovered Courtney, to her delight and my chagrin.

I was especially chagrined today not only with Courtney but also with the whole May Day mess. I always dread it when our class is chosen to participate. Dancing is definitely not one of my things. I'm taller than most of the other seventh-graders and a total failure when it comes to anything athletic. My eyes, dark brown with long lashes, are my best feature, but the rest of me is a gangling mass of arms and legs.

"You're just going through an awkward stage," my mother tells me. "This is your in-between year. You'll grow out of it."

I'm not so sure, and being the only Jewish girl in the class (besides Fern Steiner, the Great Brain) doesn't help either. Sometimes I feel like the only matzo ball in a pot of chicken-dumpling soup. So here I was, a Jewish skunk surrounded by wood nymphs and fairies, in what can only be termed a "loosely adapted version" of Shakespeare's *Midsummer Night's Dream,* this year's May Day performance.

"Girls, polka-dot yourself around the field," our dance instructor, Miss Lee, called cheerfully.

Nobody moved. It was clear that May Day was turning into a fiasco. The wired-in music was squeaky; the costumes were falling apart; the dance patterns, presumably invented by Miss Lee, were so complicated that no one could remember them. No doubt in a state of fluttery enthusiasm, she had approached the headmaster, Mr. Beardsley, who is usually unreceptive to new ideas. However, the sight of Miss Lee in her black leotards and fishnet tights must have startled him into agreeing to her elaborate plan. Not to mention the fact that Miss Elliot's thrives on English tradition—White Anglo-Saxon Protestant tradition, to be exact. The result had been two months of arduous practice, which "does not make perfect," contrary to the old maxim.

No one would consent to take the part of the two male leads except Mr. Grunwald, the science teacher, who weighs two hundred pounds, and Mr. Arnold, the organist, who tippy-toes around in a manner more suited for Hermia, the heroine, than for her lover, Lysander. The only great moment in the performance occurs when Puck, the mischievous trickster of the spirits, played by a cherubic third-grader, comes dashing out and casts a spell on Hilary Coles, the Fairy Queen, who proceeds to fall in love with Cheryl Griffith, who plays the part of a bungling actor, wearing a papier-mâché head of a donkey. How they were roped into doing those parts is beyond me. But they play the scene with such self-conscious confusion that everyone hoots with glee.

As if the pageant weren't torture enough, we read the whole play out loud in English class. One of Puck's lines has become the seventh-grade slogan. "Lord, what fools these mortals be!" we groan whenever we have to practice for May Day. Miss Lee calls her spectacle a "nonverbal interpretation" of Shakespeare, which means that the poetry is lost in the shuffle of clumsy feet and lurching bodies.

In the grand finale, the seniors parade around the field. Each girl smiles radiantly at the audience, crosses one leg behind her, and bends slowly to the ground. This is known as the May Day bow. We begin perfecting our bow in the third grade. Whenever I attempt to bow, I can't seem to get up off the ground. I feel like a newborn colt trying to walk for the first time. Wobbly legs, that's me.

Courtney is a born bower. She dips and sways in perfect form. It's no laughing matter to her, either. She's counting on being crowned May Queen when we're seniors. Everyone deserves at least fifteen minutes' worth of glory—especially Courtney, I thought, because she's absolutely convinced that she's a rare and special creature. Most of the time I feel she is special, too, but right this minute I was ready to crown her myself.

"Girls, cavort and frolic like creatures of the woods," chirped Miss Lee again.

Just as the music began for our grand entrance, Courtney, breathless and disheveled, scrambled out of the bushes and prepared to hop in iambic pentameter, which Miss Lee explained follows the rhythm of Shakespeare's verse.

"Some partner you are," I hissed.

"Just get off my case," she retorted. "I'm here, aren't I?"

"You've done it again," I had to admit.

"Ah," sighed Courtney, " 'nothing can bring back the hour of splendor in the grass, of glory in the flower' "— reciting a line from Wordsworth's "Ode," which she memorized for English class.

"It's more like 'lust in the dust,' " I said.

"Oh, we didn't do anything," said Courtney. "Scott keeps following me around. Poor kid, I couldn't just let him sit there sulking in the bushes."

"Just remember, you're a squirrel, not a femme fatale," I told her. With that, she gave me a smug smile and danced gracefully onto the meadow. Sometimes Courtney can be so stuck-up. My feet felt like buckets and my skunk's tail flapped wildly as I followed behind and tried to keep time to the music.

My only consolation was to hear Fern Steiner clumping, galumphing, and groaning behind me. Next to her, I felt positively sylph-like. She was supposed to be a rabbit.

"Carrie," she whispered hoarsely, "this is humiliating, but watching you makes me feel better." That's what I like about Fern; she can always make me laugh at myself. Side by side, we attempted the final tour jeté, a flying leap into the air.

"Watch this," I said. "I'm going to give it my all." I hurdled off the ground. Swinging my arms high over my head, I made a double looped turn. "Girls, move like gazelles, not elephants," called Miss Lee. Is that remark directed to me, I wondered, coming down for a landing. But Fern and I collided; we ended up in an ungainly pile on the grass. I could feel Miss Lee's eyes, like daggers, on my back. Heads together, Fern and I began to shake with laughter—the kind that couldn't be stifled, no matter how hard we tried. Soon we were hiccuping and slapping each other on the back. I felt a stab of affection for Fern, who is my cohort against the Miss Elliot's establishment. We always seem to have one foot in and one foot out.

As we struggled to our feet, Mr. Beardsley announced over the sound system, "Remember, young ladies, to cast your ballot for this year's May Queen. I want to impress upon you that your choice should not be governed by beauty alone but also by such qualities as kindness, gentleness, and dignity, which become a gracious ruler."

"Now, that's quaint," drawled Fern. "Where did he dig up that speech?"

"And where is he going to find a senior who's dignified?" I added.

"Queen of the May," mused Courtney dreamily. "What could be more exciting?"

"I can think of plenty of things," I said. But for a moment I envisioned myself standing on the chariot of white flowers as everyone rises to sing "Greetings to the Queen." When I make my regal entrance, the whole school showers me with roses.

"What's with that foolish grin on your face?" asked Fern, poking me in the ribs and out of my daydream.

"I was just thinking how odd it is to want something and not want it at the same time."

On the bus going home, Courtney told the driver to drop her off at Frontenac Plaza. "I need to do some shopping," she said. "Why don't you come along?"

"That's the last thing I feel like doing," I said. "I just spent my allowance at the book fair." Actually, I think shopping is a waste of time unless I really need something, but then I don't have an unlimited bankroll. Courtney does.

I discovered this undeniable fact about Courtney the

first time I went over to her house, which looks like the cover of Mother's book *Guide to the Châteaux Country*. We drove for five minutes past the main gate. First came a swimming pool, then a tennis court, and finally a pond with swans.

"My, my," Dad had said, shaking his head.

"Just don't play with the swans," Mother told me. "They flap their wings and bite." I could tell my mother was impressed by the way she looked into the rearview mirror to check her makeup.

"Oh, Mother." I remember giggling, but I felt scared when I rang the doorbell, because the house was so big.

Our family is somewhere in-between. What I mean is that we live in a nice subdivision and have everything we need, but I wouldn't go into the Record Bar after school and charge a bunch of albums or load up on Shetland sweaters like Courtney does. And we don't have a farm for weekends or a cottage in Michigan. "Tell them you 'summer' in Brooklyn with your grandparents," my dad once told me.

Dad can be exasperating, I thought as the bus jerked to a halt in front of our house. But at least he has a sense of humor.

II

Of the two, my dad is always easier to talk to than my mother, who's so meticulous and perfect about everything that she expects everyone around her to be, too. If I get a B on my report card, she says, "You should get an A next time." If I ask her how I look before I go out, she surveys me up and down and says, "Fair." Yet Dad always has a good word to say—unless my brother, Sonny, and I carry on too much at the dinner table or sass my mother. Then he's likely to grab me by the arm and shove me upstairs to my room. It's as if a huge lion were pouncing. I know it's useless to fight back; so I just stay quiet and pray it will be over soon. Most of the time, he's not strict at all.

All our relatives look up to him, because he's the only one in the clan who has made it. Dad owns a shoe factory in Flat River, Missouri, which is about fifty-five miles south of St. Louis. Mother says small towns are too provincial, so we never moved there. Instead, Dad stays in Flat River all week and comes home on the weekends. Lately he has been around more, sleeping late or just reading in his easy chair.

As soon as I walked around to the back door, I could see his car parked in the garage. What's he doing home again, I thought, slamming the back door and dumping my books on the counter. Maybe the factory's going to close down. Maybe he's out of a job. What was going on? Were my parents trying to hide something from me?

Something was wrong. Mother and Dad were sitting at the breakfast table. They were both crying. It isn't unusual for my dad to cry. He is so sentimental that he even cries at television commercials. Some of my best moments with Dad are spent weeping over some tearjerker on TV. But it is unusual to see my mother cry.

"Carrie, I can't go to May Day with you today," Mother said.

"Why not? What's the matter?" I was counting on her going. Was it just another excuse for not showing up at a school function? She thinks the teas at Miss Elliot's are like a series of bad comedy skits.

I looked over at my mother, who never sheds a tear, even when she's peeling an onion. She's not a complainer, either; yet she always seems to get what she wants. "Stubborn and strong-willed," I heard my dad mutter when she refused to go out to dinner with one of his clients.

She is also beautiful. Courtney always points to the models in the fashion magazines and tells me that they look just like Mother.

But today Mother didn't look very beautiful. Her eyes were all puffy and her dark hair was in total disarray around her face. I stood there peering around, speechless. My voice was stuck in my throat. They both looked pathetic, and I'm not used to thinking of them in that way.

"Your father has to go into the hospital," Mother finally said. "It's called the Mayo Clinic, in Rochester, Minnesota."

Minnesota, I thought. Why does he have to go so far away?

"The doctor tells me your old man is pretty sick and better get his buttocks up there in a hurry," Dad said, trying to make light of it.

But I had heard of the Mayo Clinic before. Fern's grandmother went up there for surgery last year. People go to places like that for serious reasons.

"What's the matter with you, Daddy?" I asked, struggling to get the words out.

"You're going to have to take care of your little brother while we are gone," Dad said. "We have to leave tonight. Dorothy"—that's our maid—"will stay here until we get back."

"Martin," said Mother softly, "we ought to tell Carrie what the doctor told us."

I am just like my dad about crying, but today I couldn't. I felt numb, as if something terrible was about to happen and there was nothing I could do about it.

"Carrie, come over here and sit on my lap like you used to do," Dad said.

In the past year I haven't felt much like hugging or sitting on people's laps. When I reached thirteen, that sort of thing began to feel babyish. But I went over and sank down in Dad's arms.

"The doctors say I have cancer, and if I have an operation as soon as possible, there is a good chance that I'll be all right. But the next few months are going to be difficult for all of us."

So there it was, out in the open. The room seemed to be getting smaller and smaller. Dad tightened his arms around me. I felt trapped, caged in. I couldn't breathe. My mother started to say something, but I didn't want to hear her. I just wanted to get out of there, away from their worried voices and the words I couldn't listen to.

14

"I have to call Fern and see if her mother will drive me to school," I said, wrenching myself from his grasp and dashing out of the kitchen. I quickly changed into my skunk costume and crept downstairs. I could hear my parents moving around in their room, packing, I guess. I slipped down the back way to avoid them. They were all wrapped up in their own private grief, and I felt like an intruder.

Twenty minutes later, I was sitting outside on the steps, nervously tearing my tail into shreds, when the Steiners pulled up. Mrs. Steiner always tells me to call her Gert. I think of her as Gert but I haven't been able to say it to her face yet. "What's the matter?" she asked. "You look pale."

I told her Dad was sick, but when she asked me what was wrong with him, I said I didn't know. I couldn't say "cancer," it's such a scary word. I concentrated on the road signs so I wouldn't have to think about it. I was glad when we finally were dropped off at school.

The staff went all out for May Day. There was a smell of freshly cut grass and new paint. The older girls looked so fantastical in long pastel gowns with daisy chains in their hair that I began to forget what was going on at home. The seniors, who usually run through the halls giggling and carrying on, were suddenly transformed into stately princesses weaving yellow and blue streamers around the maypole.

The "virgins' parade," as Dad calls it, wasn't a disaster after all.

Trumpets blared over the microphone. The event everyone had been waiting for was about to begin. The crowning of the May Queen! Mr. Beardsley descended from his perch on the tiers to place a wreath of white roses on the head of the new queen.

"I'll bet it's either Page Duffy or Allison Defty," garbled Courtney excitedly.

"Duffy and Defty," I snickered. "Sounds like a circus dog act."

"He sure is taking his time about it," Courney complained. Mr. Beardsley finally reached the double row of beaming seniors and stopped before Ceci Barksdale, who let out a loud squeal, hugged him, and dashed to the center of the field. Quickly courtesying, she grinned widely at the audience. A lady on the benches was jumping up and down, waving.

"That must be Mrs. Barksdale," I said, nudging Fern.

"Real dignified, huh?" commented Fern. "I think Ceci is about to lead us in a hockey cheer." Our new queen was short, stocky, and full of pep. Her dress looked like a bed sheet draped around her.

"Too bad for Duffy and Defty."

"How did she ever win?" moaned Courtney, who was clearly disappointed.

"Maybe she's a dark-horse candidate," I offered.

16

"Don't be ridiculous," said Fern, who had sized up the whole situation. "Ceci's got good old Miss Elliot's team spirit and everyone likes her."

We were all huddled on the grass with the rest of the seventh-graders. Some of the boys from Woodson Hall Prep came over to talk to what Fern and I refer to as the NOTD group. The initials stand for Not Our Type, Dearie. I suppose you would call these girls the popular set. Courtney's the only zany one of the bunch, which is probably why we're attracted to each other. Their leader, Cathy Beaumont, arches her eyebrows disdainfully whenever Courtney acts overly rambunctious. The NOTD's have a certain quality about them. If you were out shopping and didn't know who they were, you'd probably guess that they went to Miss Elliot's Academy. The first hint is their hair, which, unlike my mass of curls, is long and straight, pulled back with headbands or barrettes. I have to wear mine short, or people tease and call me Pocahontas. Sometimes I like to think of myself as an Indian maiden—dark and mysterious—living in the woods and swimming in the creeks.

And it's the way they dress, too. In the spring, most of the girls wear flowered-print Lilly skirts and pastel cotton T-shirts, with Pappagallo sandals to match. Mother tried to coerce me into buying an outfit like that a few weeks ago, but I'm not the type. I feel more comfortable in jeans and the plaid Western shirt that I bought in Aspen last year. But today I would have even worn a Lilly skirt with begonias and snapdragons instead of this silly skunk suit. There are times when I feel immense (not fat, just like a big bulk) next to the other girls, especially Cathy Beaumont, who is so tiny and delicate—not to mention her blond hair, which turns under perfectly, and her almond-shaped, hazel eyes.

"You're unusual," Mother tells me. "That will be an advantage someday." Someday maybe, but right now I'm like a butterfly stuck in a cocoon.

If I were beautiful like Courtney or brilliant like Fern, it would help, but at this point I don't seem to be very good at anything except thinking up wisecracks and dropping big words. "You have a sharp tongue," says my Aunt Miriam. I prefer to call it wit, although that's hardly a great talent to brag about. Nobody ever gets the best of me outwardly. But sometimes when the NOTD's have a party and I'm not invited or I'm the last one chosen at Fortnightly dances, I feel hurt, even though I hold it in.

"Hey, Carrie," said a voice next to me, "why are you always scowling?"

I looked up and there was Dewy Daumatt (Dumont Daumatt III, to be exact), looking his usual cool self. He lives across the street from us, and just because he happens to be junior-division tennis champion and has curly blond hair and "sexy eyes," the NOTD's are always asking me questions about him. "Did you see Dewy today?" "Does he ever come over?" Frankly, I never noticed him until this year. He was the dirty kid across the street who was always losing tennis balls in our yard. It kind of bugs me that he's become such a big deal. So I glanced up, put my hands to my forehead to block out the sun, and squinted at him as if I didn't know who he was.

"I like your outfit," he said. "Can a skunk come out smelling like a rose?"

"Why don't you do a disappearing act?" I said.

"How come I never see you outside any more?" he persisted. "I used to enjoy the disturbance you cause in the neighborhood." He was probably referring to the time I ran my bike into the Weyracks' petunias and Mrs. Weyrack came out in her see-through housecoat and started yelling at me. Dewy, who had been hitting tennis balls against the garage door, was totally fascinated by the whole event. He stood there grinning stupidly until her performance was over.

"Your bedroom window faces Weyracks'," I said. "I'm sure you get a better look at old Mrs. Weyrack that way."

Feigning shock, he said, "My, my, do you think I would ever do a thing like that?"

"I wouldn't put anything past your minuscule mind," I replied.

"Good alliteration," he remarked, "but that doesn't make sense."

"Well, at least you're not a complete illiterate."

"Say, how do you know where my bedroom is?" he said, plopping down next to me on the grass.

When Fern giggled, I noticed that some of the other kids were staring at us, especially Cathy, who likes to think of him as her boyfriend since they went together to the Woodson Hall senior play. I felt uncomfortable with him sitting right next to me and with the attention we were getting, but I decided to be as nonchalant as I could. He was obviously trying to bug me in front of everyone. Ignoring him, I pretended to watch the dancing. Finally he moved back with Cathy and the others. It's hard trying to talk to him anyway, now that he smells clean as Lifebuoy soap and looks me right in the eye. The trouble with going to a girls' school is that you're not used to being with boys, except for bratty brothers or cousins. It becomes an unusual event when you find yourself face to face with some boy at a party or at a school function. You can't talk about what So-and-so did in class or what a horrible teacher someone is, because the boy doesn't know what you are talking about. I can never think of anything to say, so I either stand there feeling gawky or I make a sarcastic remark and a hasty exit. Besides, I'm usually a head taller than most of the boys at religious school or Fortnightly dances. As far as boys are concerned, I plan to stay as far away from them as I can get, for a few years.

III

Back at home, I found Mother and Dad standing in the hall, with the bags all packed and stacked up next to them. Mother was trying to explain to my brother, Sonny, why they were going. Sonny is eight and kind of frail-looking, but when he opens a big mouth, it sounds like a cannon exploding. As usual, he was whining and giving Mother a hard time.

"Why do you have to go now?" he said, tugging at Dad's coat. "Mother promised to take me to Baskin-Robbins after school."

"The plane leaves at 7:00 p.m. and we have to get to the airport," Mother explained. I could tell she was trying to stay calm. She had a list a mile long to give Doro-thy. "Time to go, Queen Bess," said Dad, using his pet name for her.

Sonny grabbed Mother's hand. "I want an ice-cream cone," he pleaded. He was working up to his cannon roar.

"I'll take you," I said quickly. "Come on, Brat. I'll even treat you." Sonny looked appeased for a minute. Then, just as he started to protest again, Mother and Dad walked out the door.

"Take care, Carrie," Dad said, and winked at me with a kind of sad smile. That's when I felt the tears coming, but I quickly turned around and went into the kitchen, so he couldn't see me cry. I didn't want Dad to think I was afraid. I knew it would be a while before they would be back. Instead of feeling excited at the prospect of having the house to myself, as I usually feel when they go on a trip, I felt depressed and scared. What if he doesn't get better? What will Mother do then? How will we live? A lot of questions began to pop up in my head that so far I guess I had been trying not to think about.

Nothing really terrible has ever happened to me be-fore except for that time when I was in the fourth grade, and I woke up one morning with my eyes crusted shut. It turned out to be the kind of allergy that acted up in the mornings or from strong light. I was certain that God was punishing me for the time I kicked Aunt Miriam's wall and ruined her new flocked wallpaper. Every morning until my eyes stopped watering, the doctor made me wear dark glasses. I felt pretty stupid being escorted to the school bus by Dorothy with my eyes shut and sunglasses on. For a while nobody would sit next to me or talk to me. Every so often, one of the big girls on the bus would make a nasty crack like "I bet she's afraid to open her eyes and see herself in the mirror."

That's when I started acting tough—before anyone had a chance to get me first. Also, I began reading a lot at home. It was hard for me to play outside because the bright sunlight hurt my eyes. I would curl up in the library, which is a small, cozy room with a fireplace in back of the house, and spend hours devouring anything that was on the bookshelves. I read *Gone with the Wind* and *Canterbury Tales* when I was ten. After a while the allergy went away. By then I had developed a big vocabulary, which makes me even more of an oddball. "There you go with that AV [Affected Voice]," says Courtney whenever I use a new word.

I still read a lot, too. My dad's downtown office is right next to a bookstore. When he takes me there on Saturdays, I always stock up on books. I still have a couple to read from the last trip, and that's just what I wanted to do now.

But I promised Sonny that I would go to Baskin-Robbins with him. So off we went, with Sonny jabbering a mile a minute, asking me dumb questions about Dad, and me trying to be tactful and not blurt out how sick he really was.

Dewy was in the street, fiddling with his bike. "Hey, Carrie," he called, "your folks going on a trip? I just saw them leave in a cab."

"They had to go to New York for a business meeting," I said.

Sonny looked at me quizzically, but before he could contradict me, I grabbed his arm and set off as quickly as possible down the street. I just didn't want anyone to know our business—especially Dewy. He'd blab to the other kids about Dad being sick, and then everyone would start feeling sorry for me. Sometimes I wish I were invisible.

"How's the Cold Kingdom?" I asked Mr. Northrop, who was behind the counter at Baskin-Robbins. His white hair stood up as if from electricity.

"Just putting the final touches on my latest master-piece," he said, holding up a gooey purple ice-cream pie. "Grape flavor, almonds, and chocolate icing. How do you like it?"

I gulped. "Uh, it looks very interesting."

"Yuck," said Sonny. I pinched his arm.

"This is my Mother's Day special," Mr. Northrop told us. "It's coming up in two weeks."

"My mother will be gone then." Sonny looked sad

when I said that, but I didn't want to hurt Mr. Northrop's feelings by telling him what an incredible unedible he had created.

"Problem is," he said, paying no attention to me, "that I can't think of anything clever to write on it."

"How about '*Grape*fully Yours'?" I suggested.

"Say, now there's an original idea," he said, brightening. "Just for that, here's a cone on the house."

"Thanks ver*million*," I said, pointing to the bright-red cherry on top of the ice cream and feeling proud of myself.

On the way home, Sonny bit into a big clump of gum in his disgusting scoop of Bubble Gum Surprise and lost a baby tooth. "That's great," I said. "Don't forget to put the tooth under your pillow tonight."

"Carrie, tell the tooth fairy not to come until Mother and Daddy come home." Sonny sounded like he was about to cry.

"Don't worry," I said. "The tooth fairy won't forget you." I made a mental note to myself not to forget to leave a quarter in his bed tonight.

When Sonny and I returned, slurping the generous scoops of Cherry Pecan Swirl and Bubble Gum Surprise, Dorothy was waiting for us outside with her hand on her hip, looking like she was about to commit murder. Once I tried to write a short story about her, but nothing I wrote did her justice. Our housekeeper for five years, she has the room next to mine. She cleans and cooks, but mostly crabs at me. Picture a five-foot-tall bleached blonde on the chubby side, wearing a tight purple sweater and black slacks. That's Dorothy. Sometimes I'm embarrassed when friends come over and she's padding around the house in her pink mules with a perpetual cigarette hanging out of her mouth. The whole second floor reeks of her lilac perfume; yet I'm glad Mother doesn't ask her to wear a white uniform like the Allens' maid. Dorothy has the kind of personality that no one tries to tangle with except me. She has a boyfriend named Chester (Chess the Mess, I call him), who takes her out every Tuesday night. From the way she looks when they come home, I would bet that they do more than talk and go bowling. Dorothy is a voracious reader. At night, she turns on the television and props herself up in bed with her pile of paperbacks: *The Rogue's Revenge, Love's Soaring Fires,* or *Passion's Purpose.* The covers intrigue me. There's always a half-dressed lady being carried off by a burly man, usually wearing some kind of exotic uniform. Whenever she bolts up in bed and her eyes bulge out, I know she's reading an especially juicy passage. She keeps the books lined up on her closet shelf, but even when she's out, I haven't had the nerve to go poking around in there and sneak a look. However, in spite of her literary tastes, Dorothy is a great cook.

Chicken tetrazzini smothered with mushrooms in a wine sauce and hot, spiced apple pie are her specialties.

I could see by the way she was puffing up her cheeks and pursing her lips that we were in for a speech. "Okay, what did we do this time?" I asked. The way to handle the situation is to put her on the defensive first. If I keep talking, she sometimes gets flustered and gives up.

"Your parents are going to be gone for a while, and I want to make one thing perfectly clear. I'm in charge here. You two are not to go running off by yourselves without telling me what you are up to. Is that understood?"

"We were not up to anything," I said, putting my hands on my hips in a mock imitation. "I just took Sonny up to Baskin-Robbins for ice cream. Is that all right with you? Brother! I try to be nice to the Brat, and look what happens."

"Who's a brat, Frizzy Head?" Sonny interjected.

"Shut up, both of you! Let's go inside before the whole neighborhood hears you."

In the excitement, I had forgotten that we were standing on the front walk. I turned around. There was Dewy watching us. He grinned, gave me the peace sign, and sauntered inside. Would I like to catch him at something one of these days!

IV

It only took a week for the word to get out at school about Dad being sick. Everyone began to act sickeningly sweet. "Carrie, sit over here." "Carrie, walk with us to class." Instead of an appendage, I was the center of attention. Cathy Beaumont saved me a seat at lunch and even insisted on riding home on the bus with me yesterday. I had a sneaking suspicion that her sudden burst of interest had more to do with wanting to see Dewy than comforting me. Today I avoided her, because I wanted to go home alone and wait for Mother's phone call. She called once to tell us Dad was all right, but we were out. So far, I haven't even received a postcard from her.

I missed my parents, but in a way it was like a holiday since at night Mother wasn't there to tell me to practice my piano or do my homework or wash my hair. I spent the last two nights rummaging around in the basement, where Mother keeps mementos in big cardboard boxes. She saves everything. I've always loved sitting on the cement floor looking through her old letters and photographs.

Instead of a phone call, there was a letter waiting for me in the mailbox. "Dear Family," Mother began. "The operation is over. Dad needs to recuperate here for a few weeks. Will call soon. We love and miss you." She added a hasty, scrawled signature at the bottom. Why was her letter so short? Why didn't she write more about the operation? What a frustrating disappointment! She could have at least told us about the weather, or the food, or about anything, instead of two noncommittal lines and the usual "love and miss you."

"I'll bet she called Aunt Miriam," I grumbled to myself. Then I remembered how helpless my parents looked, hunched over the breakfast table on May Day. I squeezed my eyes shut to block out that image, but I couldn't.

I ran downstairs to the basement and pulled out their photo album from the carton loaded with souvenirs. I wanted to find a picture of Mother and Dad in another time, another place. The room smelled moldy from decaying books and clothing. The first photograph I came across was one of Mother and Aunt Miriam standing in front of a huge ocean liner, the *Queen Elizabeth*, about to sail for Europe. Soon I was absorbed in all their old souvenirs. I could hear Aunt Miriam's voice describing that long-ago trip as if it were yesterday, as if it were the greatest moment in her life. I often wonder how Uncle Mike feels about that. Everywhere they went, she claims men were attracted to my mother. They were wined and dined all over Europe. There are pictures to prove it: Mother on the beach, her hair blowing in the wind, in a French café with some guy's arm around her, or in front of an expensive-looking foreign car. I don't know if she intended me to find these remnants of the past, but it's like piecing together a puzzle. I've started a scrapbook for my children, but so far there's nothing much in it but some matchbooks from our vacation in Colorado and a Rolling Stones autograph.

Then I came across the most enticing souvenir of all—a stack of old letters stuffed in a mildewed carton. Without hesitating a second, I tore off the blue ribbon and ripped the first letter out of its envelope. My eyes nearly popped out of my head—love letters from an old boyfriend. Overflowing with sticky words such as "Beloved" and "Angel," they revealed the moaning and groaning of somebody named Melvin Philpot. "Elizabeth, I'm pining away! When are you moving to New York?" I cannot imagine anyone suffering over me that way; it'll probably be just the other way around.

I put the letters aside and began to dig further. A series of photographs were scattered loosely at the bottom of the box. The best picture was crumpled in a corner. I finally found what I had been searching for. Mother and Dad must have been at a nightclub. They were dancing and looking starry-eyed at each other. I laughed out loud at Dad's funny profile.

Mother didn't marry Dad until she was thirty-one, because she was head of an advertising agency. She told me once that in her day it was unusual for a woman to rise to such a high position. I can't blame her for not wanting to give it up. Dad, who had moved to St. Louis from Brooklyn, was so persistent that she finally gave in and married him. But she didn't quit her job until after Sonny was born. Now she does freelance work for department stores. Occasionally she even designs shoes for Dad's company. He's always bragging about her to everyone. According to Dad, "Elizabeth can make the most ordinary product bubble like champagne."

Dad started out as a salesman for a large corporation here. At night he worked in the basement of their apartment developing a new kind of leather sole, but the company he worked for stole his design. According to my Uncle Mike, when Dad sued them it became a landmark case, and he was able to open his own factory with the money from the settlement. There is a leather-bound book of the trial: "Singer [that's us] versus Boonshaft." Although most of it is jargon and impossible to read, I thumbed through the pages and almost memorized the things that Dad said on the witness stand. He sounded so sure of himself. Sometimes I think my parents were much more interesting when they were young. They both grew up in poor families who immigrated here from Russia and Hungary. Their households spoke a mixture of English and the Yiddish they occasionally lapse into when they don't want Sonny or me to know what they're talking about. When Sonny flunked the Woodson Hall entrance exam on purpose, they spoke Yiddish for a week.

Sending me to private school and belonging to the country club is a big deal. It always makes me nervous to go to the Club (as my mother refers to it) with her. Mother puts on this charming act, smiling and embracing all sorts of strange people. She's never demonstrative about showing affection at home. That's why I bristle when I see her lavish attention on casual acquaintances. I don't mind when I see Mrs. Steiner rolling around on the floor tickling Fern's little brothers. That's a different kind of touching. They're being affectionate because they really love each other. But I stiffen immediately when a friend of Mother's tries to hug me at the club. I wonder what I'll do if a boy ever tries to kiss me?

I hate those phony gestures in public places. Mother

32

has never come right out and said that, but I sense by the expression on her face that "You do things because it is expected of you" is an unwritten law. Sometimes it helps to watch a person's eyes when they speak to me. If they have a blank or faraway look, that's a sure sign that they don't mean what they say. Lately I've been avoiding people's eyes, because I think they're feeling sorry for me.

I stared at the photograph of Mother and Dad for a long time. I could tell that the sun was going down, because the light through the basement window was fading. I carefully put the yellowed envelopes and photos away and went upstairs to pester Dorothy about dinner.

V

With the sound of nonstop barking and the rumbling of a busted muffler, the Steiners' Volkswagen bus screeched to a stop. Gert, who behaves more like a pal than a mother, was waving inside.

"Piano lessons," she called. "Hop in." Gert has been especially nice since my parents left. Although she never asks a lot of questions about Dad, she invites me for dinner and drives me around. Gert is so different from my mother. She never makes remarks like "Young ladies don't behave that way," or "Never speak to strangers." Maybe that's why Fern is so unusual. I love my parents, but I sometimes wonder what it would be like to have Gert as a mother.

She always wears jeans and a faded workshirt, even at PTA meetings. The customary outfit for mothers is an A-lined, monogrammed dress. My mother, of course, sweeps in, swirling her crimson cape like a bullfighter, her gold bracelets jangling, her stiletto heels clicking across the floor. The other mothers seem to fade and disappear into the woodwork when she enters a room. However, if *Popular Mechanics* had a centerfold, Gert would pop out. She's a potter, so there are always chunks of dry clay stuck in her hair or under her fingernails. One of her favorite subjects is the girls and their parents at Miss Elliot's. The only thing Gert has in common with Mother is their distaste for school functions.

"Dreariest group of suburban snobs I have ever met," she began as I climbed over Jasper, their German shepherd, who was drooling in the front seat. Then she launched into an account of her latest faux pas at Miss Elliot's. "I spilled tea all over Mr. Beardsley today. When I tried to wipe it off, I splattered clay dust on his suit."

" 'Mah deah Mrs. Steiner,' " she continued, mimicking his Eastern accent, " 'how clumsy of us . . . pahdon me.' I never saw anyone walk away more quickly. If Fern wasn't the smartest kid in the school, I'm sure we would have been booted out long ago."

Dr. Steiner, a professor of art history at Washington

35

University, thinks that Fern is receiving a better education at Miss Elliot's. He insisted that Fern needed a private school, despite all Gert's protests. Besides, they gave her a fat scholarship, so the Steiners don't have to pay a cent. Gert figures that if she pulls enough outrageous stunts and brings up controversial subjects like drugs or sex at meetings, they won't renew Fern's scholarship, so she can go to public school with the rest of the family. I hope that never happens. I don't know what I'd do without Fern. Gert keeps telling Dr. Steiner, "It's absurd to treat Fern differently because she's a genius."

Dr. Steiner just nods and continues puffing on his pipe and reading *ARTnews*. If you ask me, I think all the attention has made Fern self-conscious. That's why she's so shy at school and refuses to sit with the other kids at lunch.

"I hate all that dumb talk about boys," she says. "But you go ahead, Carrie. I don't care." Then she clenches her thumb in her fist, starts munching on her sandwich, and ignores me. What a pain she can be! She's always saying she doesn't care. But I know she does, and I feel guilty about leaving her sitting there all alone.

Mother likes Fern because she knows she's smart and figures it might rub off on me. So far, it hasn't. But she has decided that "Gert is trendy." Dad enjoys teasing Gert. "What's the latest cause this time—marching for abortion, or passing pills out to teenagers?" he asks with a grin. If anyone else (especially Dr. Steiner) talked to her that way, she would get furious, but Dad has a way of making her laugh. They knew each other at New York University. Ever since they ran into each other again on family night at Miss Elliot's, Dad's been teasing her about leaving New York for the Midwest.

"Martin," she comes right back at him, "you've become stuffy since you made all that money. Pretty soon you'll be paunchy like the rest of those businessmen and rock your way to old age on the ninth hole of some country-club golf course."

As Gert shifted gears, curving around a bend in the road, Jasper landed in my lap. He licked my face but wouldn't budge.

"Where's Fern?" I asked, elbowing Jasper out of the way.

"In the science lab at school. She's working on splitting the atom again," explained Gert.

"Haven't you told her about Einstein?" I joked.

"I wouldn't want to stifle her creativity. But if you hear a loud explosion coming from Miss Elliot's, you'll know why."

"Something to look forward to," I said. "Tell her to call me later, and thanks for the ride." I slid over Jasper and eased myself out of the car.

Fern is just the opposite of her mother—quiet and intense. The first time I ever saw her was last fall. She was standing on the corner waiting for the school bus, wearing a strange green-and-pink printed tent dress that made her look like an overgrown watermelon pickle. Her light brown hair was in long braids, which is definitely out for a seventh-grader. Later I discovered that tent dresses are all she will wear, because she thinks she's fat. Gert makes them out of any bizarre print that she can find. The wilder, the better. I don't think Fern notices the fabric; it's the style that she's obsessed with. Mother once suggested that we all go shopping together, but I told her if she ever mentioned it to Fern, I'd be furious.

Fern blushes easily and has a habit of laughing at the wrong times, especially when the gym teacher, Miss Beaner, is trying to explain a hockey play. The Beanpole, who is six feet tall and never smiles, only likes the athletic girls. If your family happens to be socially prominent, that doesn't hurt either. Fern and I are off her list on two counts.

Fern and I got together out of desperation last fall when the Beanpole stuck us on the bench during hockey intramurals. Except for the fact that we both avoid taking a shower after gym class, we didn't think we had much in common. Showers are one of the Beanpole's rules. I manage to run down to the lockers and peel off my smelly gym suit, which hasn't been washed all year, before she can check up on me.

Fern whizzes down there even before I do. The only

one who doesn't mind showering in front of everyone is Courtney, who likes to show off her bust. Besides, her long blond hair doesn't frizz up like mine. Courtney would make a great model for a shampoo commercial.

"The Beanpole's a real pain," I can remember saying to Fern as we sat there on the bench shuffling our feet. I was relieved not to have to run up and down the field, but I did feel out of it. Fern just squinted straight ahead, as if she were really watching the game.

"She's probably got a complex about not being married," I continued.

"Well, I'm never getting married either," snorted Fern, screwing up her nose at me. I would have given up on her right then and there, but the defiant look on her face and the way she held her hands in a fist made me curious. "What do we need to be jocks for. Let the horsey set run their you-know-what's around the hockey field. I'm going to improve my mind."

That remark finally produced a response. Fern let out an exaggerated sigh. "Well," she said, "what's a nice Jewish girl like you doing in a place like this?"

"Are you Jewish, too?" I asked, pretending to be surprised. I knew she was, because of her last name. In a school of Van Fleets, Norfolks, and Rands, Steiner and Singer stick out like a sore thumb, but Mother tells me it isn't polite to ask people things like that. I was glad she brought it up, though.

"Welcome to the club," I said, thumping her on the back.

"Who else is in the club?" asked Fern.

"Two people," I said. "You and me."

Discovering Fern on that hockey bench was one of the best things that ever happened to me at Miss Elliot's.

VI

Fern and I sit together every day during chapel services. Slumped in our seats Friday morning, we were people-watching. Miss Elliot's Academy was started by an Episcopalian minister who insisted on chapel services every morning, and now, even though the school is nondenominational, chapel has become a tradition. Wearing green-and-gold blazers and blue pleated skirts, the lower-school girls marched in, two by two, to their appointed seats. How close they are to the rostrum depends on their age. The big girls were the last to straggle in. Ceci Barksdale pranced in, flanked by her admirers.

"She'll never look like a queen," muttered Fern.

"Why is she still wearing that stupid crown?" I asked. "The flowers are all dried out." We stared at them enviously.

I can't wait to get to the stage when I can casually strut down the aisle to my front-row seat, I thought. The final person to enter was Mr. Beardsley, who always dons a long, black robe and walks stiffly up to the podium as Mr. Arnold blasts out a Bach processional on the organ. I wish he would just once substitute a rock version of it. Mr. Beardsley announced grimly, "We will now bow our heads for the Lord's Prayer."

I could hear Courtney's voice coming from the row in front of us. "Our Father, *wart* in heaven, *Halloween* thy name. Thy Kingdom come, thy will be done, on earth *adjectives* in heaven." She's been saying it that way since the first grade. Until the service was over, I sat and daydreamed, watching the sunlight filter through the long, oval windows.

For two months now, Mrs. Swallow, the middle-school director, has been reading *The Lion, the Witch and the Wardrobe* after the first hymn is over. It's about four children who walk into a closet in an old house and find themselves in a mysterious, magical kingdom. I used to imagine myself falling down a rabbit hole like Alice, or passing through a door into my own secret world—a world of curious creatures and crazy characters. I could see myself twirling around and around, moving from one adventure to another. I have read all the books in the series, but I'm never bored hearing the story again. Mrs. Swallow stands up there on the podium looking prim and severe, with her gray hair pulled back tightly in a bun and her spectacles balanced low on her nose—an intellectual prairie dog. But when she opens her mouth, she gives a completely different impression. Her voice, which is low and melodious, assumes the role of each of C. S. Lewis's characters—especially the lion, whose roar fills the room and reverberates off the walls. Because of her, chapel has become something to look forward to.

The part that makes me angry is that we have to attend whether we want to or not. My parents don't care, but Gert keeps calling the school to protest, especially after the Christmas program, when Fern sang "Adestes Fideles" dressed in a long white gown with silver angel wings attached to her shoulders. I think it was the tinfoil halo that really set Gert off. When Fern insisted on wearing green for St. Patrick's Day, Gert went berserk.

I can remember when we walked into their house after school and found her fuming around in her studio. "This is the last straw," she shouted, picking at her clay-caked bangs, "seeing two little Jewish girls dressed up like a leprechaun and the Jolly Green Giant." Fern and I promptly hopped up on her workbench and sang a chorus of "Holy, Holy, Holy! Lord God Almighty."

"Out of here," Gert shrieked, waving a paintbrush in

the air. Fern and I stumbled out of the room, doubled over laughing.

Sonny, who was sent to public school after Woodson Hall refused to accept him, doesn't know anything about Christian holidays.

"It's against the law to teach religion in our school," he announced proudly. "Mrs. Ambruster, my music teacher, says we should learn about that stuff at home."

"Well," I told him smugly, "when I sing Christmas carols, you don't even know the words."

"Who cares?" he replied.

"You have an indolent and lackadaisical attitude," I said.

"What was that?" he asked, shaking his head. I ended up teaching him some songs, so we could entertain Dorothy on Christmas Day. She always gets depressed, being away from home on holidays. Anyway, I think kids should have the fun of knowing about other people's customs. And how can you avoid Christmas? The stores put out their decorations in November. At Miss Elliot's, we started singing carols in October.

Fern and I decided they should give equal time to Hanukkah, my favorite Jewish holiday. We approached Miss Ames, our class advisor.

"I suppose it would be all right," she told us. "But you two girls plan everything."

Fern lugged the family menorah to school the next day and set it up next to the Christmas tree. I put in eight candles. The whole seventh grade was invited to the service. Even though it was a free hour, everyone showed up. Fern lit the candles with the shammes while I sang in Hebrew.

"Ba-rukh A-to A-do-nai E-lo-hei-nu Me-lek Ha-o-lam," I began. "Blessed art thou, O Eternal, our God, King of the Universe."

I was really surprised when the other girls started asking a million questions. Why don't we believe in Jesus? What's going on in Israel? What is the story behind Hanukkah?

Fern explained that we believe that Jesus was a great teacher but that Jews do not think that he is the son of God. She spoke in her firm but quiet little voice, and I knew everyone was really listening to her. I felt proud of her, of being Jewish, of having something special to share with the girls.

Courtney asked, "Do you really get to open presents eight nights in a row?"

Cathy said, "I bet you'd convert just for that."

Everyone laughed.

There have been moments like that at Miss Elliot's that shine as brightly in my memory as those Hanukkah candles last winter. And then there are those other moments when Miss Elliot's Academy seems like a wax museum that I wish would melt away—along with Mr. Beardsley, the NOTD's, and my math teacher.

"I'm glad tomorrow's Saturday," I told Fern as we filed out of chapel. "I'm leaving my books in my locker on purpose."

VII

"This place looks like a cyclone's hit it." Dorothy had been ranting and raving around the house all weekend. I could hear her squawking as I was pulling off my nightclothes. For the last week she's been following a laissez-faire policy, but the mess was beginning to affect her. Then I noticed a brown stain on my pajama bottoms; I didn't know what it was from. I pitched them in the wastebasket so Dorothy wouldn't find out and take me to the doctor. She's always poking around in everything. I was really panicky, positive I'd caught some awful disease.

By noon Dorothy found the pajamas. I was hiding in

my room. There was a "Do Not Disturb" sign on the door, but she didn't even bother to knock.

"Just walk right in," I muttered, burying my nose in my math book.

"Has this ever happened before?" she asked, holding up the pajamas.

"I don't think so," I mumbled. I knew my face was turning red.

"Hasn't anybody ever told you about menstruation?" she asked.

"Of course," I said. "I know what that is. We had a film in school last year."

Then suddenly it clicked. Boy, did I feel like a nitwit. My mouth kind of dropped open, but before I could utter a sound, Dorothy said in a very businesslike way, "Here, I think you might need these. Come to my room if you want any help."

Then she handed me a package with some pads and a belt in it and walked out of the room. I was glad she didn't laugh or joke around about it. The mystery was solved. I felt relieved, and excited, too. Everyone at school is always talking about getting the curse, but not many girls in seventh grade have gotten it yet. I wanted to call Mother right away and tell her, but I couldn't reach her in Minnesota. I'd wait until tomorrow to break the news to Fern so I could see her face when I told her.

The best part of the day at Miss Elliot's is lunchtime—

mainly because of the food. By eleven-thirty Monday morning, halfway through math class, I started glancing at the clock. As soon as the bell rang, there was a frantic dash downstairs to be the first in line. The cafeteria is a large, multi-purpose room with round, white Formica tables, blue carpeting, and hanging baskets in the windows, the only section of the school that has ever been remodeled. My favorite lunch is creamed chicken with biscuits and a cherry cobbler for dessert. The tuna casserole with potato chips sprinkled on top and the roast beef with mashed potatoes and gravy aren't bad, either.

Dorothy keeps trying to get the tuna recipe from Miss Elliot's cook, but she won't divulge her secret. Dorothy's tuna casserole consists of one can of tuna fish mixed with Campbell's cream of mushroom soup. Ugh! She has served it three times since Mother and Dad have been gone.

"Engage Bertha in a conversation so I can grab an extra corn muffin," said Fern, who was saving me a place in line. Bertha, Miss Elliot's cook, was guarding the muffins as if they were the crown jewels.

"Forget the muffin," I whispered. "I have more important subjects to talk about."

Fern wrinkled her eyebrows. "There's nothing more important than my nourishment."

"Let's sit alone in the corner," I insisted. "If Courtney finds this out, she'll start shrieking and carrying on."

49

"Guess what?" I demanded in a superior tone.

"You passed a math quiz; you're moving to Afghanistan; a boy called you."

"No! Better than that," I said. "I got my period." Then I leaned back in the chair to watch her reaction. She emitted a loud series of squeaks, followed by "You're kidding!" After a long pause, she frowned. "I bet I'll never get mine. Wait till I tell Gert."

"Don't mention it to her yet. I haven't even told my mother."

"You know what this means?" asked Fern in a low, serious tone.

"What?"

"You better watch out or you could get pregnant." Then she chortled in a high-pitched, witchy way that made me laugh.

I was glad to be sharing my secret with her, but I missed Mother and I felt an ache inside, remembering Dad's sad smile when we said goodbye. I stared down at my plate. The corn muffin stared back. I pushed the plate away.

Fern must have sensed the change in my mood. Taking me gently by the arm, she said, "Why don't we go sit outside by the creek until French class?"

I know I complain a lot about Miss Elliot's Academy, but there are some special features about the place. For one thing, there is the creek in back that goes under the highway. If we are caught playing in it or wandering away from the school, it's an automatic suspension. I have a lot of fantasies about doing that, but I just don't have the guts. Courtney once waded under the tunnel all the way to Clayton Road and pulled the caper off. But she's one of those people who get away with everything. My luck, I would fall into the creek, straggle back to class dripping wet, and be sent home immediately.

We walked through a small grove of trees, across the May Day meadow, and down to the creek, which was rippling with water after the spring rain. There were violets spread out like a purple carpet all along the edge of the creek, which winds its way clear around Miss Elliot's. I breathed in and out deeply, cupping my hands in the cold water and letting it slip through my fingers. In the distance I heard the last bell signaling afternoon classes, but it was a while before Fern and I started back to school.

VIII

Tuesday was Dorothy's night to go out with Chess the Mess, and I was stuck baby-sitting with Sonny. We were outside playing catch and screaming at each other, when who walked out of his front door and across the street but the great Dumont Daumatt III himself.

"Hey, you guys, toss the ball to me," he called to us.

I wanted to tell him we were busy, but Sonny, who thinks Dewy is the greatest on earth, got all excited. "Don't have a spasm," I told Sonny. His tongue hung down like a festival banner. "You mean it, Dewy?" he said. "You want to play with us?"

"Sure, kid." Dewy grinned. "Come here and I'll show you a throw that your sister will never catch."

Sonny went trotting over eagerly, while I sat down on the grass and stared at them with what I hoped was amused indifference. After a while, Sonny grew tired of practicing and wandered off.

"How's your dad?" Dewy asked, looking down at me. He was wearing a blue polo shirt that matched his eyes, and I had to admit that he was good-looking.

I was sure that Dorothy told his yardman about Dad, and that was how he found out. "Oh, fine," I said. "They will be home right before school is over." He was the last person I felt like talking to about it.

"Hey, why don't we walk over to Baskin-Robbins and get a cone," Dewy said.

I couldn't believe it! He never had asked me to do anything with him before. I guess he was being nice because of Dad.

"I have to watch Sonny tonight," I said. But I wanted to shout "Yes!"

"Well, sure," said Dewy. "Sonny can go with us."

I just sat there a minute, looking at him with a foolish grin, because the next thing he said was, "You've got a nice smile, Carrie. Come on, let's get Sonny and go."

On the way, he told me all about his big tennis match with the top player from Community School. He had already won the first three sets, and they were scheduled to play again tomorrow. "I wish I could play a sport like tennis, but I'm so bad at all of that," I said.

"Oh, it just takes practice," he said. "Besides, my dad was state champion in college and he's been working with me since I was seven. I think he'll kill me if I don't win tomorrow."

He looked kind of worried, so I changed the subject and started talking about the Woodson Hall bus driver who keeps going over our grass every morning when he turns the corner. Sonny kept interrupting with "Look at this, or look at that" to Dewy every time he saw anything that caught his eye, which was every two minutes. Dewy and I had to laugh at him; Sonny can be so silly sometimes. I was starting to feel comfortable with Dewy and wondered if any of the other girls in the neighborhood had seen us walk by. It was fun walking next to him, bumping elbows. He is about two inches taller than I, so I didn't have to stoop over, as I usually do with boys.

At Baskin-Robbins, I hesitated before ordering one scoop of vanilla ice cream instead of my usual three. I didn't want Dewy to think I was a pig.

"Don't tell me you're worried about your weight with those long legs?" said Mr. Northrop, winking and giving me an overdose of whipped cream. I felt a creeping hot sensation on my face. I read in a magazine once that if you stand with your legs touching, they should form a figure eight. But when I stand that way in front of the mirror, I remind myself more of a pretzel.

"Carrie, take a look at my newest *pièce de résistance*." Mr. Northrop produced a bright green ice-cream pie, complete with an array of peppermint sticks protruding out on top. "My Memorial Day Special! I'm planning ahead."

"Looks super," said Dewy. I shot him my "You've got to be kidding" look when Mr. Northrop turned.

"Can you think up a name for it?" asked Mr. Northrop. Quick-thinking Carrie—but my mind went completely blank. I stood there digging my sneakers into the linoleum floor. Then, just as we were walking out the door, an idea came to me. Poking my head around the corner, I called out, "How about U.S. Govern*mint*?"

"Thanks ver*million*," answered Mr. Northrop. "You'll go far in this world."

"How did you think of that?" Dewy asked.

"Didn't you see the lightbulb flash on in my brain?" I said, grinning.

We shared his banana split and sat outside on the curb eating and watching the cars go by. It was starting to grow dark, and the air smelled of honeysuckle, which lines the street.

"I love this neighborhood, especially when everything turns green in the spring," I said in a half whisper to myself.

"Yeah, I wouldn't like living in the City," said Dewy. "I just spent a week with my cousins in New York at Christmas—all those cars and people running around made me nervous."

"It's a nice place to visit, but I wouldn't want to live there," we started to say at the same time, and then both started laughing. He reached over to grab the cherry out of the ice-cream dish, but I popped it in my mouth first. We looked at each other and laughed again. I knew this was really happening—laughing and talking with a boy so easily—but somehow I felt that a part of me was standing back and saying, "Hey, Carrie Singer! This isn't really you." It was very strange. Part of me knew he was just being friendly and that was all, but I almost wished he would hold my hand on the way home. Now I was going to have something else to start daydreaming about in chapel. Boy, life was getting complicated!

Maybe now that it's springtime and school is almost over, some good things will start happening. Maybe Dad will get well; maybe I'll have a boyfriend; and maybe my bust will start growing—maybe that's too many maybes to want all at one time.

IX

Disaster struck Miss Elliot's Academy! Head lice! Friday morning, the nurse examined everyone's hair in the whole school. We stood waiting for our turn in the hall. For head lice to break out at Miss Elliot's is comparable to going to a costume party dressed as a ghoul and showing up on the wrong night.

Cathy Beaumont walked out of the nurse's office smirking. She walked past Fern and me like we were Dracula's daughters. "I guess she's all right," I said. "We're next," mumbled Fern. The nurse poked around in my hair for five minutes. Her uniform was so white it was almost blinding. She finally let out a huge moan. "I found one," she said. "You're the thirty-fourth case."

"Are you sure it's not dandruff?" I asked. The look on her face was one of alarm tinged with disgust.

"Here's a slip to excuse you from classes," she said in a resigned voice. "Don't come back to school until the nits are gone." She handed me a bottle of Kwell shampoo and motioned me out the door. I don't think I'd like to have her job.

"Well, at least we miss a half day of school," I told Fern.

The Sunday morning newspaper announced that head lice was a suburban epidemic. Even Woodson Hall Prep was mentioned. When I called Fern, Gert answered the phone. She was ecstatic. "Shakes all those hotsy-totsys up a little bit," she said. "But after yanking forty eggs from Fern's head, I now know what the expression 'nitpicker' means."

"Your mother is at least good-natured about it," I told Fern. "My mother regards the whole thing as a personal affront." She had already called three times. Dorothy had orders to go through the house like a tornado, rip up everything in sight, and haul it off to the cleaners. Anything that couldn't be carried out (the beds, couches, tables, Dad's easy chair) Dorothy sprayed with the vilest-smelling stuff I've ever encountered, next to Aunt Miriam's cabbage rolls. Mother even threatened to come home for a day to check on us.

As soon as Fern and I hung up, the phone rang again. It was Mother. This time she wanted to remind us to shampoo our hair every night, take our poodle, Pippin, to the dog groomers, and throw out all hairbrushes.

"Can I just talk to Dad?" I asked impatiently. I needed to hear his voice, to reassure myself that he was all right. Mother always tells us he's sleeping when she calls. But this time she gave in.

"Carrie, what's this I hear about lice?" came Dad's voice through the receiver. "I can't leave you alone for a minute." He sounded just the same. We talked for ten minutes. I told him all about school. "I know this is a dull question, but how's your math?" he asked.

"Miss Cosgrove, our math teacher, makes a face every time I ask her to explain a problem. All she can say is, 'Don't bother me, I'm in a bad mood.' "

"I'm in a bad mood, too, cooped up in this hospital," Dad said, "so I sympathize with her, cooped up in a classroom all day."

"What about me?" I asked. Dad chuckled.

"Will you be home before school's out?"

"Look for me around the end of May," he answered. "And, Carrie, don't worry about this lice business. Mother's overreacted. She's turned into a picker. There's not a plant in this room that's safe now. I even caught her examining the nurse's hair and flicking lint off Dr. Stone's white coat." I tried to imagine Dad's face smiling into the phone.

"Queen Bess says it's time, Carrie. Goodbye, I'll see you soon."

The rest of the day dragged on. Sundays could be so boring. I started writing in my diary, but my pen felt like it was glued to the page. I called Fern and Courtney. Fern had gone out. Courtney wasn't home either. I poked around in Mother's dressing room. I even tried on the long black gown she wore on their anniversary. The neckline drooped down to my waist. Revolting. I spat at my reflection in the mirror as the dress slid into a silly black puddle around my feet. There must be something I can do with myself, I thought, staring down at my hairy legs. Suddenly I realized that without Mother home to say no, I might as well experiment. I rifled Dad's medicine cabinet until I found a razor. I then proceeded to massacre my legs. Unfortunately, I got blood all over the towels, and had to crisscross six bandages up and down my calves.

There's no question about it. I've reached puberty, but the only way my body seems to be changing is vertically. I wonder if I'll ever stop. My nose is growing longer, along with my feet. "Spring is busting out all over," mainly on my face, which seems to sprout a new bud every day. I figure the only way to deal with it is to be poetic; however, between the goop I blob on my face that television ads "guarantee effective," the bandages on my legs, the frizzing up of my hair, and head lice, I feel like some kind of creature from another planet. I was declaring myself in a state of emergency when Sonny bolted through the door. "Doesn't anyone ever knock in this house?" I shrieked.

"All you ever do is stare at yourself in the mirror," Sonny taunted. "If I were you, I'd give up. Once a gawk, always a gawk."

I threw my brush at him and got him right in the stomach. The way he hollered and carried on, Dorothy thought I had maimed him for life.

She screamed at both of us. "With your dad in the hospital and everything, you would think you would at least try and act human. I'm disgusted with both of you and I'm sure your mother will be, too, when she gets home."

Frankly, I didn't care. I'm sick of everybody right now and don't feel like acting "human." And the whole scene with Dorothy standing there in her hair curlers and faded flowered housecoat, Sonny lying on the floor bellowing, and the dog running around yipping at our feet struck me as so hilarious that I burst out laughing. This made Dorothy even madder. Her face turned red as an overripe persimmon, and tears streamed down it. That was when I began to feel terrible, but I was too deep into it to back down; so instead of saying "I'm sorry," I stalked out of the room and slammed the door. Then I turned my electric blanket on 10 and curled up under the covers. I felt really guilty and kind of afraid about what she would tell Mother and Dad when they got home. Sometimes I hate the way I act. And there's really nobody to talk to about it.

Fern goes to a shrink every Saturday morning. Gert's into all that Freudian stuff and thinks if Fern plays those stupid psychology games with her analyst she is acting out her aggressions. Fern says when she was younger they would sit there all morning and play with dolls and draw pictures. Now she talks and Dr. Dingwald asks leading questions and grunts every once in a while.

"Sometimes," Fern told me, "I think he's nodding off to sleep."

"Well, your life isn't exactly the *Tales of the Arabian Nights*," I commented. I would rather just talk to somebody who's not trying to figure me out or analyze but who really understands and would be sympathetic.

I heard Dad tell Mother one day that every time anybody has one little problem they go running off to a psychiatrist. "Total self-indulgence," he said, "and a damn waste of money."

"But most of the people we know are doing it," said Mother.

"And that's just the reason not to," said Dad. "If a

family has problems, they should work it out themselves and not depend on someone who, just because he has some degree on the wall, thinks he knows all the answers."

Maybe Dad was right, but there's a shadowy place in my mind that pictures myself wandering around in circles. Once I saw some elephants parading at the circus, holding each other's tail. They seemed to move slowly, mindlessly, for hours. I wondered if they would lumber round and round forever. Finally, someone had to come and lead them off. Maybe I need another person to help me out of my rut, too. I reached for the diary under my pillow to make a list of "Prospective Persons to Talk to." Blank page!

X

Sonny and I were summoned to Aunt Miriam's for dinner on Dorothy's night out. I didn't want to go because my cousin Ilene, the family star, would be there. To say that we dislike each other would be putting it mildly. She's either been ignoring or harassing me since I was five. Ilene was sitting in the family room, totally absorbed in polishing her fingernails. Mother says she likes to take good care of herself. Ilene didn't bother looking up when we came into the room. Just because she happens to be smart, sophisticated, and beautiful, the rest of the family adore her. But that's not the reason I don't. You could say our relationship is summed up by a remark she made to me when I was about ten: "I have two favorite flavors of ice cream, two favorite uncles, and two favorite cousins. You're not one of them."

Her parents always buy her one scoop of vanilla and one of chocolate; her uncles compete for her affection; her cousins follow her around like puppy dogs. I pretend she's got measles and stay out of her way. Ilene was her usual charming self that night. Just as Aunt Miriam was about to serve brownies, indicating dinner was almost over, and I was wondering if it would be too rude to go home immediately, Ilene sauntered over and crouched down beside my chair.

"Now that your dad's sick, I guess I'll have to be nice to you," she said, tossing her red hair back like a lion's mane.

"Don't bother," I replied. "You might overexert yourself." Ilene bristled like an insulted peacock—all long-necked indignity. She deserved it!

The phone rang. It was Mother calling Aunt Miriam long-distance again. I finally grabbed the phone and asked her if I could skip the Fortnightly dance that was coming up.

"No, Carrie," she said. "We signed you up and you should go."

"You always make me go to those horrible parties. I hate them," I shrieked at her. I almost knocked the phone off the table. "The boys are pimply, scrawny fruits."

"Now, Carrie," Mother said in that slow, patient tone she always uses, that never fails to aggravate me. "You might be surprised and have a good time."

"I never have a good time. I always sit in the corner until Mrs. Henderson drags some drip over to dance with me, and it always turns out to be someone too short, so that my chin rests on the top of his head. I'm not going." Then I hung up on her.

Fortnightlys are a humiliating experience. All the decent boys have paired up with the NOTD's. My mother doesn't understand this. To her, being invited to Fortnightly is a social feather in her cap—certainly not mine. She thinks I'll develop "social poise."

Fortnightly dances (by invitation only) take place in the assembly room of the Wydown Church. The girls line up on one side of the room, the boys on the other. When Miss Henderson blows a whistle, the boys dash over to grab a partner.

The crowd thins out, and guess who's left sitting there? I wish I could take a potion to make myself shrink like Alice in Wonderland. The music begins; some reluctant boy, propelled by one of Mrs. Henderson's meaningful glares, says to me, "I guess I'm stuck"; and everyone begins dancing. First comes the box step, then the waltz, the cha-cha, and finally, after punch, we all start doing the hustle. Miss Henderson usually dashes about bellowing instructions and threats, but by the time punch is served, no one pays any attention to her. Then the boys start throwing cookies. They zing them all over the room. Last month a macaroon knocked Mr. Henderson's toupee off. That's when I went and hid in the cloakroom until it was all over.

Gert thinks "it's all a bunch of garbage," but she makes Fern go, too. Fern doesn't mind, although she won't admit it. She dances with the same boy every time —a real jerk named Harmon Wesselman, who is supposed to be some kind of mathematical wizard.

Anyway, after I slammed the phone down, Uncle Mike grabbed me by the arm and dragged me into the living room. "You know your father's very ill, don't you?" he said, standing so close that I was having trouble breathing. I nodded. "Well, if something happens to your father," he went on, talking very loud and fast, "your mother will be all alone to take care of you. And if you keep on being rude like you were over the phone, we are going to have to take you away from her."

I looked up at him, this hulking six-foot-two brute with his menacing face and cigar-smelling breath, and said, "You're an insufferable boor." As he sputtered and gasped, I walked out the front door and all the way back to my house in the dark. It was only four blocks, but I was so angry that it seemed like two miles. The trees were like dark, menacing ogres about to reach down with their craggy limbs and grab me. I rushed into the house and collapsed on my bed. I vowed I would never speak to Uncle Mike again.

Five minutes later, he came over and tried to talk to me, but I wouldn't open my bedroom door. There is something deep inside me that refuses to kowtow to people like that. I must have inherited it from my mother, who is obstinate, too.

Then Uncle Mike's sister, Shirley, the "blond bombshell," called to apologize for him. "You know your mother and dad paid for my wedding," she said in a placating tone, "and Mike feels he owes your parents a lot. He's really devoted to both of them."

"Well, he sure doesn't know how to show it," I told her.

"He was just trying to get you to cooperate a little more. You're not exactly easy to get along with. I know it wasn't right of him to threaten you like that, but he didn't do it maliciously."

"That's what you think," I answered. "Anyway, I don't want to talk about it any more. Just keep him away from me." And I slammed down the receiver.

XI

My relationships with people seem to be going from bad to worse these days. I just can't help it. Friday after school, Gert gave Fern a birthday dinner at their house, and I had what Dorothy would call "one of my temper tantrums." The evening started out fairly smoothly. I always love being in the Steiners' crazy menagerie. They live in a broken-down Victorian town house in the middle of the city. Very few people from Miss Elliot's live in that area, because most of the surrounding streets are blighted, with vacant, windowless houses, and the buildings are being torn down. Gert is always saying, "Everyone is afraid of being robbed, but we have never had any problem. All the families who stick it out here are very close and supportive. If anyone ever tried to break in, I would understand it, because of the way people are treated in this city."

Some of girls refused Fern's invitation, because their mothers were worried about the neighborhood. But there were enough people who accepted so Fern didn't feel too badly. Also, the three floors of mahogany-paneled rooms are fun to roam around in. Most of the girls have never been inside an old city house filled with cubbyholes, secret nooks, and crannies.

Gert was her usual crazy self. When we all trooped in, she said, "Well, girls, how does it feel to be in the inner city? Have any of you ever been east of Warson Road?"

"My grandmother used to live around here," said Courtney, "but she says that the whole area is run-down now." Then she covered her mouth with her hand and looked embarrassed.

Gert cringed a little but said, in a very controlled way, "You're right, Courtney, this used to be the grandest area in St. Louis around the turn of the century. But wealthy people began moving to the suburbs. They were afraid of living with people who were different than they were." Gert was sounding so formal. I was glad when Fern said, "All our neighbors are black."

"My parents wouldn't like that," said Courtney, "because Grandmother wouldn't like it."

"Well, you don't have to be that way, do you, Court-ney?" chimed in Fern's little brother. Now Courtney looked confused.

"Come on, girls," said Gert. "Fern will show you the rest of the house. I'll see about supper."

Then, when everyone started commenting about their cactus collection and the wild pillows from India which are piled up to sit on instead of couches, Gert said, "See, ladies, there are other ways of decorating besides flow-ered chintz." Fern groaned, but it went right over every-one else's head.

The only room in the house that has any order about it whatsoever is Dr. Steiner's study, which is floor-to-ceiling bookshelves, with manuscripts and notebooks all ar-ranged in meticulous order. "It's the only room I refuse to clean," announced Gert. Everyone looked around with a puzzled expression, because there was nothing out of place, and the rest of the house is in complete chaos. Gert has an easel set up right in the middle of the living room, because, she explained, "that's where I can get the best light."

The downstairs is filled with large abstract paintings by Dr. Steiner's colleagues at the university. We were standing around peering at an eight-foot vinyl ham-burger in the hallway when he strode in, puffing absently on his pipe. "What's this supposed to mean?" Courtney, bold as ever, placed her hand on the shiny sliced pickle that topped off the sculpture. For a moment Dr. Steiner looked aghast, as if she had startled him right out of a profound thought. He cleared his throat. "Well, girls, what else does this remind you of besides a hamburger?" Silence. Everyone looked at him like he was crazy. Finally I ventured a response. "How about a big bed or a cushion to jump on?"

"Excellent, Carrie," he said, nodding his approval. Silence again.

Dr. Steiner continued puffing. The smoke curled up around his face like a gray veil.

"I know," said Courtney. "It's like a giant beret with a green tassel." Then everyone started playing the game, walking around the hamburger, poking and whispering.

"You see, modern art is not an Abominable Snowman," Mr. Steiner concluded as he marched grandly into his study.

Fern said, "Dad thinks the hamburger is the pivotal image of twentieth-century American life."

"Speaking of hamburgers," said Courtney, "I'm starved. Let's eat."

We all sat around their butcher-block kitchen table for dinner, which consisted of bean-sprout salad, a corn and tomato casserole, and taco chips. Gert is not the world's greatest cook. We sat there taking dainty bites, trying to be polite. Gert was completely oblivious, and so were Fern and her little brothers, who kept shoveling the corn concoction in their mouths as if this were their last meal. In the middle of my trying to swallow an unidentifiable lump from the salad, Courtney asked me how my father was getting along. That's when I fell apart. I swallowed hard, glared at her, and ran out of the kitchen into the bathroom, slamming the door. I can't stand it when people talk to me about it. Fern started knocking on the door.

"Go away!" I yelled at her. "I'm okay." I don't care what they say to me, no one is going to see me crying or carrying on. Why is it that someone's sympathy can make you feel so terrible?

When I finally emerged, everyone was very quiet and looking down at the floor or up at the ceiling. I just wanted to get out of there and back to the safety of my electric blanket. Then Fern's brother, Joshua, spilled his Coke all over Courtney's silk skirt and she started screeching. Everyone clambered around her to sop up the liquid, and my doldrums were temporarily forgotten.

XII

The end of May was finally here. My parents had been gone almost a month. When I came home from school, I saw Aunt Miriam's car parked in the driveway. I knew Mother and Dad were back. My stomach felt jumpy and my hands were all clammy as I walked into the house. I didn't even bang the back door.

Mother was waiting for me in the kitchen. She hugged me. It was like being brushed by a feather. She was wearing a light green suit with a flower pinned on the jacket.

"Carrie, let me look at you," she said. "How are you?" I could tell by her voice that she wasn't mad at me for being rude on the phone.

"Fine," I said. "Where's Dad?"

"Upstairs, and he's eager to see you."

I raced up to their bedroom, which is the prettiest room in the house. There are two bay windows and the curtains and bedspread are a blue-and-yellow flowered print. It is always filled with sunlight. Today the shades were drawn.

Dad was sitting in bed with his briefcase open and papers strewn all over. Aunt Miriam was fidgeting around the room with that stiff-upper-lip expression on her face.

Dad's hair was grayer, and he had lost a lot of weight. He looked so much older. I bent over to kiss him. He smelled of soap and medicine. He pulled me close to him and hugged me hard for a long time.

"I missed you so much, Carrie," he told me. "How's school?"

"All right, I guess," I said. I was afraid to tell him how badly I was doing. He would find out soon enough when report cards came out. There were only ten days left of school. "It was kind of hard to concentrate."

"I can understand that," Dad said. He started coughing and spitting up in a handkerchief. Aunt Miriam ran over to see if he needed anything, and I ran out of the room.

I felt all mixed up. I didn't know if I was glad that they were home or not. Everything was different.

The doctors told him he could come home from the hospital as long as he promised to stay in bed. In the evenings I could hear him coughing. It doesn't sound like a regular cough but more like a loud gasp from deep down in the stomach. Sometimes his coughing fits lasted so long that I had to hold a pillow over my head to drown out the sound. I couldn't stand to hear it, so I tried to be away from the house as much as possible. When he asked me to come in and talk to him, I lasted about five minutes. Once I told him what I had for lunch, who I sat with on the bus, and how much homework I had, I took off. I told my friends not to come over, I didn't want to have to explain about Dad. I wasn't sure what I would say.

Now that people know he's home, a steady stream of my parents' friends have been coming over, offering words of advice and bringing novels, layer cakes, board games, and plants, which he hardly notices. Sometimes Mother's friends stop by before going to a party. I can tell she feels sad by the way she "ooh's" and "ah's" over their clothes and hair. The worst part of it is the way they talk to me—trying to be cheerful and sorry at the same time. I want to scream, "Go away! He's fine, he's not going to die!" I keep wishing he would wake up feeling better one morning and this would all be over.

Mother insists that I answer the door and entertain

guests until Dad is ready to see them. Sometimes he comes down in his robe, but most of the time they go upstairs to his bedroom. I hate to watch their faces when they see him for the first time.

One night, Linda Ring and her parents came over. She is a year ahead of me at Miss Elliot's and without a doubt the prettiest girl in the school. She's tall, with long black hair and green eyes. She looks and dresses just like her mother. She had on three-inch heels and a halter dress; so did Mrs. Ring. I guess they spoil her because she's an only child. Everyone likes Linda because she's so sweet —like Karo syrup, if you ask me. She sat downstairs with me in the living room while her parents went up to talk with Dad. I kept looking at her and thinking, Doesn't anything terrible ever happen to you? I bet she's one of those people who will go through life without a care in the world. Gert always says that people who suffer are stronger for it, but when I looked at Linda Ring, I wished I could do without some of that suffering.

"My mother was sick for two months last year," Linda was telling me.

"I didn't know that," I said. She probably had the flu, I thought to myself. I didn't feel like sitting here watching Linda Ring in her halter dress and spiked-heel shoes practice paying a sympathy call.

"She had a mastectomy," Linda said.

"A breast operation?" I said, stunned. Mrs. Ring is so pretty. I suppose that really bothered her. "Gee, I'm sorry."

"Don't be sorry," Linda said, very matter-of-factly. "At first she was upset about losing one breast, but now she's glad to be alive."

It's easy for you to act calm and casual, I wanted to shout in her baby-doll face. Your mother's not the one who's lying upstairs sick in bed. I swallowed hard. I was in awe of Linda and resentful of her at the same time.

Time to change the subject fast, before she reduced me to tears. "Oh-uh-so what are you doing this summer?" I asked, as if I really cared.

Linda looked at me with a very steady gaze. "Carrie, I really hope your dad gets better. If you ever feel depressed, please call me. I know how awful it is and no one ever wants to talk about it." Linda was right.

"Thanks," I said and I meant it. I take it back about the Karo syrup.

XIII

I had a terrible day today. I'm a mess, my face is all broken out, and I flunked a French quiz. Also, Miss Ames, who is my advisor, called me into her office. She is one of the younger teachers in the school. A lot of the girls copy the way she dresses and wears her hair. She was graduated from Miss Elliot's and then went to Radcliffe. Mr. Beardsley always points to her as the perfect example of a "Miss Elliot's girl." She reminds me of Saran Wrap—thin and transparent. She was sitting at her desk, holding a copy of my report card.

"Your grades have all dropped this quarter, Carrie," she said. "I hate to see this happen. You were doing so well." I knew she expected me to explain it to her, but I didn't know what to say. So I just sat there looking down at my lap. "I know this has been a difficult spring for you because of your father," she went on. "That probably has a lot to do with it."

I wondered how she heard about Dad and what that had to do with my grades. It's for sure that I didn't want to talk about it.

"Yes, I guess so," I mumbled. I knew if I said anything I would start crying. I could feel my voice faltering and the pressure building between my eyes. I kept telling myself, "Just don't let her see you cry." So far, I haven't cried in front of anybody, and I wasn't going to now. That's all Mother and Dad needed was to hear I was crying and complaining about things at school.

She said a few more encouraging things like "Remember, you can't get into a good college with grades like this." I excused myself and left. I wanted to go home and hide in my room with my books and records. It seemed like hours before the bell rang so I could get on the bus and leave. Sometimes I have nightmares about running out of the school just as the buses pull away and not being able to stop them, or that I get on the wrong bus and get stuck on the other side of town. That's why I'm always the first one on the bus.

Fern wanted me to come over and see their new German shepherd, but I didn't feel like it. I was also in a bad mood because I hadn't talked to Dewy since that night we had ice cream. Cathy Beaumont, who writes his name all over her books, said he called her last week. That's what I get for starting to care about somebody. It was probably silly to even think he would notice me anyway. I always look for him when the bus turns the corner. Sometimes he's outside in the back yard, but I haven't ever had the nerve to walk over and talk to him. Sonny goes over there, but I'm afraid to ask if Dewy ever mentions me. Today I was feeling so bad that I figured, what did I have to lose? I might as well just walk right over there and be friendly.

He was sitting on the back steps talking to Eddie Doyle, who lives in back of him. Oh, no, I thought. What am I going to say now, with Eddie standing there? I stumbled over a rock in the driveway as I walked toward him.

"Hey, Carrie," Dewy called, "how have you been? I called Cathy the other night to see what was going on with your dad." I looked down at the ground. "You've been running into your house so fast lately that I figured you didn't want to talk to me."

I wondered why Cathy hadn't bothered to mention that to me. "Well, I've had a lot on my mind," I told him.

Eddie Doyle said, "Why would she want to talk to you anyway, big shot?"

"Aw, go home, Eddie. I'll see you later."

We just stood there looking at each other for a minute. Then suddenly, I don't know why, I burst into tears.

"Come on," he said, and walked me over to the big elm tree at the end of his yard. We both plopped down under it and I cried for a few more minutes. Despite my determination to hold it in, the tears seemed to spew forth like hot lava from a volcano. Dewy didn't say anything. I wondered if he was embarrassed by my blubbering all over him.

"My dad is really sick," I finally said, looking over at him. "I want him to get well but I can't do anything to help. Nobody tells me anything, but I know he's not getting better." I started crying all over again. When I cry, my nose gets all runny and my face puffs up. I knew I looked terrible. I started sniffing and wiping my face on my sleeve.

"Here, use this," said Dewy, handing me an old wadded-up Kleenex. I blew my nose. After a while, shoulders touching, we sat with our backs against the tree trunk. Dewy said slowly, "My grandmother died three years ago. She lived with us since I was two, so I was pretty used to having her around. She always told me stories at night about her family in Holland, and every day after school she had fresh-baked chocolate-chip cookies waiting for me. I didn't realize how much I missed her until after she died. I went to visit with her once in the hospital, but the way they had her all doped up turned me off and I never went back. Then she died and it was too late."

"I know what you mean," I said, thinking about Dad upstairs in his bed coughing and moaning. "I try to stay out of his way as much as I can. I don't know what to say or what to do."

"After she died," Dewy continued, "I thought about all the things I wanted to thank her for but didn't—like the cookies, and the scarves she always used to crochet that were too long, or when she stuck up for me if Dad got on my back about grades or tennis."

For a while we just sat there listening to the birds and to the voices of kids yelling up and down the streets. For the first time in weeks I felt that I was with somebody who understood what I was feeling—even if it was a boy I didn't know very well. I looked over at him for a moment and he opened his eyes and smiled. All of a sudden he jumped up and gave a loud whooping shout and climbed up the tree. He swung his leg over a limb and hoisted himself up into the branches. Then he looked down from between the leaves and leered at me. "Come on up," he said.

Oh, no, I thought. Right in the middle of the first peaceful minute I've had outside of my electric blanket for weeks, this idiot wants me to climb a tree. "I can't," I said aloud.

"Why not?"

"I just can't."

"Try it. Here, I'll help you. If you get to the top, you can see all the way down to the Arch."

"The great Gateway to the West," he boomed like a television announcer. "Yes, folks, it's 630 feet high—a huge arc made out of shining steel." The Arch was designed by a famous sculptor named Saarinen. It's down by the river and looms up high over the city.

"I don't believe you," I said. "The Arch is too far away from here."

"Come on up. I dare you."

"Listen, if I climb up there, fall down, and break my leg, it's going to be your fault." Sometimes I think that words can do more to kill you than anything else. I know a girl whose brother was dared to jump off the roof of his garage—and it was his friend calling him chicken that broke his head open, not leaping off the roof. Anyway, why should I have to prove myself to Dewy? What did I care? And I could imagine how I would look, trying to pull my body up that tree.

"No, thank you," I said, and started to walk away. Then Dewy gave another whoop and jumped down right in front of me. "Here," he said, "take my hand and I'll hoist you up. It's just the first step that's hard. The rest is easy."

So I let him lead me back to the tree, and before I

knew it, I was straddled on the limb helplessly, holding on to the branch for dear life with one hand and grabbing on to Dewy with the other. I could feel the gnarls of the bark digging into my thighs. It was scary, because I knew if I lost my balance, it would be all over.

"Now just put one foot up in front of you. Let go and grab on to the limb above you. There, that's it. You have more balance than you think you do."

I could feel myself perspiring, but all of a sudden I knew I just had to do it. With one quick movement, I swung my leg up and reached for the branch above me. And there I was, standing in the V of two branches, and looking down at Dewy, who was grinning up at me.

"Bravo," he said, laughing.

"I think that's about the bravest thing I've ever done," I said. Then I remembered that time in Michigan when my friend's father took a bunch of us to climb the forest ranger's lookout tower, and I got halfway up, panicked, and came running down. Mr. Carp told my dad later that I was less spirited than the other kids, who had gone racing up to the top, laughing, without a care in the world.

"Carrie's plenty spirited," my dad had said. "She just was a little afraid of the height. Happens to me all the time."

But, standing up in the tree, I didn't have the dizzy feeling that I sometimes get in high places.

"Come on up," I said to Dewy, who swung himself up in a single movement, and soon we were clambering up the branches to the top. "Hey, you can see the Arch from here," I cried. And there it was, glimmering in the distance, the buildings downtown reflected in its surface. "I don't think I'd ever want to go up inside it," I said. "It's much better as a piece of sculpture to look at or walk around. Most people just want to ride to the top for the scenic view." Dewy didn't say anything to that, but I could tell by the way he looked at me that he had never thought of the Arch that way before, and he liked the idea.

The next problem to overcome was how to get down from the tree. Dewy scrambled down easily, swung from the lowest branch by his knees, and somersaulted to the ground. I have never thought of boys as being graceful, but he has a certain ease about the way he moves. I'm envious of that, and all the dancing lessons in the world are not going to loosen me up, at least not right now. Every move I made was awkward and uncertain as I tried to get down from the tree with Dewy peering up at me. Luckily, I was wearing my gym shorts under my skirt; I had finally decided to bring them home to be washed. When I made it down to the bottom branch, Dewy held out his arms and said, "Jump and I'll catch you." The very idea of jumping right down into his arms struck me as funny and frightening at the same time.

"I'm too big," I said. "I'll kill you."

"Well then, jump yourself. I'll give you two minutes, or I'll have to call the fire department."

I burst out laughing and then jumped down, landing in a heap at his feet, which was far better than landing in a heap on top of him.

The sky was turning pink and violet as the late-afternoon sun went down. I felt so good I wanted to jump up and down and throw confetti. Now I couldn't wait to get home and run upstairs to talk to Dad. No more avoiding him, I told myself. There are too many things that I want to tell him.

XIV

Recently, Dad hasn't even had enough energy to get mad at Sonny and me when we start fighting. I'm not afraid of him any more, but I don't know how to talk to him the way I used to. But I went upstairs to his room anyway to give it a try. He was propped up in bed, surrounded by his pill bottles, tissues, and business papers, which were scattered all over the bed. The room had that medicinal odor that reminds me of doctors' offices. He took his glasses off when I walked in, and said, "Carrie, come sit down on the bed. I haven't seen much of you lately. What's going on?"

I started to tell him about climbing the elm tree, but I was still feeling secretive inside about Dewy. I wasn't ready to share that yet. Instead, I began to complain about the party I was going to at Courtney Allen's. "All the couples are going. I'm the only one who doesn't have a boyfriend, but Courtney invited me anyway."

"There will probably be other kids there without a special beau," said Dad, patting my hand. "What do you do at those parties?"

Since this was the first small party I have been invited to, I told him I really didn't know. "But I suspect everyone will want to turn out the lights and play kissing games."

"Well," he said slowly, "now don't you be too easy to kiss, Carrie. Boys really don't like girls who are."

"Oh, Dad," I answered, "you sound like the rabbi at temple. Anyway, I'm not worried about kissing, I just hope someone talks to me."

"You'll do just fine," he said. "And if it doesn't turn out exactly the way you want it to be, just remember that your father thinks you're the greatest. Why, the whole world is your oyster and one of these days it will open up and you'll find the pearl."

The party started at eight o'clock Saturday night. I arrived at ten after eight. Fashionably late, I figured. No one was there yet. Courtney was skipping around, all excited. I thought she looked terrific in yellow slacks, with her face flushed pink.

"Guess who's coming," she said.

"Cathy, Andrea, and Linda," I answered.

"No, the boys, stupid."

I knew she meant the boys, but I didn't want to sound overeager.

"I can't imagine. Who?" I asked, hoping Dewy was going to show up.

"Everyone neat except Dewy." She gave me a knowing look. "Are you disappointed?"

I didn't answer.

"Cathy is," said Courtney, "but Dewy is in a tennis match tonight."

She put a tray of potato chips on the coffee table. Her basement was as long as the house, but it wasn't anything like ours, which is filled with boxes and cast-off furniture. There were two couches next to a big fireplace. On the left was a pool table; on the right was a soda fountain. I looked around for a chair. It was in the corner. I always look for a safe spot, just in case.

The rest of the girls came together. Cathy smelled like Fabergé perfume. They were all wearing jeans. I had on my winter Fortnightly jumper. Mother had said, "You ought to dress up when you go to the Allens'." That was the first bad sign. The second was B. J. Deggendorf, who said, "Hi, Pocahontas," when he saw me. The third was

Tully Topping, who suggested that we all pair up and play the "Disappearing Game."

"What's that?" asked Courtney.

"You find a partner and disappear," he said.

"Dumb idea," said Courtney. "Let's dance."

Three more boys came. They played pool. The rest of the kids danced. B. J. Deggendorf danced as if he were trying to dislocate his knee joints. I sat on my chair in the corner and flipped through *True Confessions* and an Archie comic book—neither of which I usually read. Finally I walked over to change the record. I was getting tired of "Disco Fever." I noticed a few people playing the "Disappearing Game."

Oh, no, I thought, panicking. Roger Baker was heading my way. Dull brown hair, straight, and flapping like a patch over one eye. I looked down at him. He looked at me.

"Wanna sit?" he asked, pointing to the couch. There's only one word for Roger—slimy! That was when I zoomed to the phone and called Mother to come pick me up. I slipped out the basement door, crashed into the garbage cans, and groped my way up the stairs in the dark.

"How was the party?" Mother said when I got into the car.

"Okay, I guess," I answered.

"It's so early. I remember my first party," she said

91

gaily. "We danced all night, but I was seventeen. You're lucky to be going to parties so young."

"Yeah, real lucky," I snapped. She didn't ask me anything after that.

When I reached home, relieved to be away from the scuffling and heavy-breathing scene going on at Courtney's, I said to Dad, "Well, if the world's my oyster, it was sure clamped shut tonight."

He laughed and hugged me, saying, "Baby, you're going to be a beauty someday." The funny thing is that I feel deep down inside that he's right. It's just going to be a long wait before I'm discovered, and that's the pain of it.

Dad sat up in bed. "Carrie, how about a midnight stroll?"

"It's the middle of the night, Martin," said Mother.

"All the more reason to get out of bed. I've always been a night owl. Besides, I'm going to have bedsores from all this lying around." With that, Dad emerged from under the sheets and put on the blue silk robe Aunt Miriam bought for him.

"You're going outside in that?" Mother chided.

"You're right, Elizabeth," said Dad, winking at me. "I need to be properly attired for a date with my best girl." Disappearing into the closet, he poked his head out a moment later wearing a black top hat and holding a silver walking stick. He offered me his arm, tipped his hat to Mother, and off we went.

For June, the air was unusually fresh and cool. The moon was full, hot white, and hung simply in the black sky. All around us was the sound of crickets and starlings singing. I smelled the night-blooming jasmine. We didn't say very much at first. We just listened to the sounds and walked slowly past Dewy's house, the Weyracks', and across to the empty lot on the corner. I wondered if Dewy won his tennis match.

"Let's sit down for a minute," said Dad. There was a bench next to the street lamp.

"Are you feeling any better?" I asked him.

"Some days are better than others. Right now, I feel wonderful, being out in the fresh air on such a beautiful night with you," Dad said. "I've always loved summers in St. Louis, but the heat really does me in now that I'm sick."

"I'm scared sometimes when I hear you cough," I told him.

"I know you're worried," Dad said, pulling me close to him. "I'm frightened too, but at least now I know what's really wrong with me. For a long time I had stomach pains and didn't know why."

"When you feel better, can I go with you to the factory?" I asked. I've always loved playing around with the typewriter and cutting out patterns on the machines.

"You know, Carrie," said Dad, "for so many years I worked constantly to build up my business, to provide the best for you and Sonny. Staying home these last few months, spending more time with your mother, I realize how lucky I am to have my family."

"Dad, you can always find something good in everything," I said, shaking my head. I didn't feel lucky at all.

"Let me tell you a story that my grandfather, the rabbi, once told me. Maybe now is the right moment. Once upon a time," Dad began, "there was a king who owned the most precious diamond in the world. One day, as he was boasting and displaying the stone, the king discovered a huge scratch on its surface. Summoning the most expert diamond cutters, he proclaimed: 'A chest of gold for anyone who can repair my damaged stone.' But no one could remove the scratch from his once-perfect jewel. One day an artist came to the king with promises that he could make the diamond even more extraordinary than it had been before the accident. The king gave it to him out of desperation. Several weeks later, just as the king was about to give up, the artist returned to the palace. With great skill he had etched a lovely rosebud on the diamond. The scratch was transformed into a graceful stem. My grandfather always told this story to people in his congregation who were ill or having hard times. 'When life wounds you,' he would say, 'remember the artisan who turned scratches into something beautiful.' "

"I love your stories," I said, putting my head against his shoulder as we walked back to the house. "I wish I had known Grandfather Singer."

"Well," said Dad, "now you know him through me. When I tell you some of the things he used to say, it brings back so many images and helps me remember him."

XV

When I went over to Courtney's this morning, she started
giving me all kinds of advice about how to act with boys.
"You just can't sit pouting in the corner all night waiting
for a boy to talk to you first. You have to smile more and
be friendly," she told me. "Besides, you have perfect
teeth." She grimaced and tugged on her braces.

"I'm not changing my demeanor for a bunch of infan-
tile boys," I grumbled.

"There you go with all that old AV," she said, laughing. "Really, Carrie, you're more fun to be with than
anyone I know. Why can't you just loosen up a little
around other people?"

I told her I try but it doesn't work.

"Well, you have to try harder."

She was getting on my nerves. I wasn't going to admit to Courtney that sitting in a corner wasn't my idea of fun, either. "Why did you invite that slob Roger, anyway?" I asked.

"I didn't. He just showed up and we had to make the best of it."

Courtney has the typical American "give 'em a good time" attitude. She is so bouncy that it looks like she's on springs when she walks. She is the original Sunshine Kid.

"It's that will-to-happiness syndrome," says Gert. "If the Allens had been on the *Titanic* when it was sinking, Courtney would be looking up at the sky saying, 'Well, the ship's going down, but isn't it a lovely day.' Her problem is that she's fifth-generation St. Louis. There's nothing like a little Russian blood, like we have, to give you a good sense of doom and gloom."

Maybe being fifth-generation does mean a lot to the Allens, but I don't think they put on airs. When Gert starts on that subject, she sounds like a broken record.

"The whole family looks like they just stepped out of *Good Housekeeping*," she once complained. Whenever she sees Mr. Allen in his tweed jacket as he walks their basset hound, Homer, she makes a loud harrumphing snort. But Mother loves the way Mr. Allen dresses. She always notices things like that. Last fall she went out and bought Dad the most outrageous pair of Scottish-plaid pants she could find.

"Thanks, Queen Bess. I'll wear them to the next wine-and-cheese party at the hunting lodge," was Dad's reply. He puffed on an imaginary pipe and strutted around in the slacks, which were way too long and rolled up at the bottom.

"I guess you're not the type," Mother said, sighing. Then she looked over at Sonny in his spaghetti-stained shirt and at me in my faded jeans. "It's up to me to add a little style to this family."

When I got home from Courtney's, she was wearing a red hostess gown with a bright green sash. Even though she and Dad are home all the time now, she always dresses up.

"It keeps Martin from getting depressed," she told Aunt Miriam, who was sitting with her. "I don't want him to see me slopping around looking gloomy. Although the way he languishes in bed all day, I wonder if he notices."

I remember another one of Rabbi Singer's stories from the Talmud—about a sailor's wife who put on her best clothes every day while her husband was at sea. When friends asked her why, she replied, "Something could happen. If he comes home earlier than expected, I want to be prepared and look my best." I wondered if this was Mother's way of preparing herself for something.

Her lip started to quiver and Aunt Miriam began bustling about the kitchen, yapping about Ilene's latest feat. That always seems to cheer Mother up. Ilene is one of their favorite subjects. If I told her I climbed a tree, I'm sure she wouldn't be impressed. Still, I was grateful to Aunt Miriam. I don't think anyone in the family, especially me, could stand to see Mother step down from her pedestal. It would be like Humpty Dumpty falling off the wall. I feel like a cracked egg myself most of the time. I wonder if the pieces of my life will ever fit back together again.

XVI

Sunday night—miracle of miracles—Dad had a sudden burst of energy and talked about going out to dinner tomorrow night. "This will be my great leap of faith," said Dad, making the effort to climb out of bed. He grasped the bedpost to catch his balance, and Mother rushed over to help him. "It's more like a limp of faith, isn't it, Elizabeth?" he said to her. "Well, everyone get out your best duds. I am going to treat you to a night on the town."

"Do we have to go?" whined Sonny, who has an aversion to changing his clothes more than twice a week.

"Come on, old kid," said Dad. "I'm going to take you out in polite society tomorrow."

"This ought to be a riot," I said. "The last time Sonny went to a civilized place to eat, he unscrewed the tops of the saltshakers, tripped the waitress, and managed to stuff himself with three hot-fudge sundaes."

Sonny stuck out his tongue; Mother laughed. She was moving around the room in an almost waltz rhythm, pulling clothes out of drawers and glancing in the mirror. I grabbed Sonny's hand and steered him out of the room.

"Listen, Brat," I said. "This is the first time they've gone anywhere for months besides to the doctors. You just better act decent or you'll be sorry. We're lucky they want us to go with them at all."

"Big deal," said Sonny as he went into his room, but I knew he understood what I was trying to get through his thick skull.

Going out on the town must mean the club, I thought to myself, surveying my meager wardrobe, which, aside from Levi's and Miss Elliot's uniforms, consists of one striped dress, a velvet jumper for Fortnightlys, and a peasant skirt that Gert brought me back from Guatemala.

"Carrie," Dad called, "go out with Mother and buy a new dress."

Shopping is low on my list of priorities, but I decided to take Dad up on his offer. So, Monday afternoon,

Mother and I drove over to Famous-Barr department store to look for a dress.

"Carrie," she said, "we don't have too much time. Let's try to find something here so we're not running all over town."

"What if I can't find anything here?" I said. "Nothing ever fits me right, anyway." I really wanted a new dress, but I had a feeling that anything I'd like, Mother would say was tacky or too expensive. We took the escalator up to the second-floor junior shop. There was a slogan on the wall:

> *You're too old for tots,*
> *You're too young for teens,*
> *You're just a gal who's in-between.*

An ominous sign, I thought, running to keep up with Mother. She was walking quickly ahead of me to go through the racks. She has a low tolerance level in big stores, and I could tell she was impatient before we had even begun.

"Awful," she kept saying as she flipped through the dresses.

"Here's one," I cried, reaching for a cream-colored peasant skirt with a flowered top.

"Well, go try it on," she said. "Here, take this one,

too." She handed me a plaid jumper that reminded me of one of Fern's tent dresses.

"I don't like that," I said.

"Try it on, anyway," she said in a very deliberate voice. "You can't tell unless you try it on."

As we were standing there, Courtney walked by with Mrs. Allen. Courtney was wearing a pink skirt with a matching scarf.

"Courtney," my mother said, "what a wonderful color on you. Carrie, look at Courtney's skirt."

"Mother," I said, "I'm going now to try this on." Whenever Mother tells me to look at the way someone else acts or dresses, I feel that she's saying, "Carrie, why can't you be like So-and-so." I wanted to tell her to shut up, but I didn't want to make her angry or we would end up going home with nothing.

I shut the curtain in the dressing room and made sure it wouldn't slip open. Pulling my jeans off, I wondered if she would like the outfit. It's hard, trying to pick clothes out by myself. I'm always afraid I've made the wrong choice. The skirt was just right; and so was the blouse, except for the fact that you could see right through it. I was sure Mother would have a fit. But when I walked out of the dressing room, she said, "Perfect! I love that on you."

"Mother, you can see my bra. It's too sexy," I told her.

"Nonsense, you look very zippy." She turned to the saleswoman and said, "Here's my charge card. We'll take that."

"Mother," I protested, "I can't wear this." I was getting exasperated. There was a whole rack of blouses that would work better with the skirt. But she was eager to go home. The saleswoman just stood there, her head going back and forth from Mother to me as we glared at each other.

"All right, Carrie," she said with a resigned sigh. "Try something else on with the skirt. We have a little more time. I guess you are old enough to pick out your own clothes. Besides, I trust your taste. You come by it naturally." She stationed herself on the chair by the dressing room and waited another hour while I tried on almost every blouse in the store. I finally picked out a blue peasant blouse and a sleeveless white shirt. I was skipping as we walked out of the store. I said to Mother, "Thanks for letting me get these things. Do you really like them?"

"Your father will be proud of his family tonight," she said, smiling. I knew that was about as far as she would go in giving me a compliment.

XVII

As I dressed for dinner, I began to conjure up visions of the feast that would be lavished upon us tonight. Going to the club is predictable all the way from gobbling oysters Rockefeller to being accosted by Mrs. Llewelyn Wasserman, a country-club fixture and a nosy old biddy besides. One of the few ways to get through an evening there is to be completely gluttonous and oblivious to anything else.

The club is a quasi-English Tudor manor house—a cross between Wuthering Heights and the Bastille. The first members probably told the architect, "Design it so that it looks like there's been money in the family for years."

"Well, I'm ready for anything," I told my reflection in the mirror. I loved the skirt, which was full, with a ruffle at the bottom.

We all gathered downstairs for the royal procession to the club. Mother was radiant in a beige linen long skirt and silk blouse; Sonny looked slovenly in shades of navy blue and gray (his one and only outfit); I looked my usual awkward self. And Dad, well, Dad looked better in pajamas than in the droopy suit he was wearing now. He must have seen the dismayed look on my face.

"Dahling," he said, feigning an exasperated grimace, "now that I've lost all this weight, I simply haven't got a thing to wear."

"Martin, you're still the handsomest man in the world," said Mother, holding on tightly to his arm as we made our way out to the car.

Some royal procession. We looked more like a band of straggling misfits, except for Mother, who is always resplendent.

When we walked into the club, my parents were immediately surrounded by friends, who clustered around them buzzing like bees. There was a lot of laughing and hugs. I saw worried looks exchanged, too, but there was something nice about going to a place where everyone knows you—a sense of belonging—for my parents at least, and I felt good about it.

Sonny and I went back to the buffet table so many times for crab meat that Mother pretended to be embarrassed. Dad didn't eat much, but he and Mother talked and whispered together. It would have been like old times, except that Sonny and I were on such good behavior that we didn't bicker, and Dad, despite his jovial mood, looked tired and restless by the time we managed to roll our way toward the dessert table. Mother came up to Sonny and me as we were testing the different pies and cakes. The waitress was giving me bites from a spoon, but Sonny bypassed that by using his index finger.

"Children, do you mind if we skip dessert? Daddy has had enough celebrating for one night. I think he should go home to bed."

Sonny started to protest, but my warning look stopped him. Reluctantly, licking the whipped cream from his fingers, he followed us out. Mrs. Llewelyn Wasserman caught us just at the door. She is a gargantuan figure of a woman, with a booming voice that demands to be heard. Yet when she began to ply Dad with questions, Mother stood up very tall and still and looked at Mrs. Llewelyn Wasserman in such a way that she seemed to shrink in size and finally just backed away. Faced by Mother, she had about as much presence as invisible ink.

We drove home in silence, but it was the kind of silence that comes from feeling very comfortable and relaxed. Sonny's head was on Dad's lap, and Mother drove. I was half asleep when we pulled in the garage, so I went right upstairs to bed. I vaguely remember Dad coming into my room and kissing me good night, his warm hand on my arm.

I awoke in the middle of the night to the murmur of strange voices upstairs and a lot of thumping around. When I walked out into the hall, I saw two men carrying a stretcher up the front stairs. I could hear Dad coughing in the deep moaning way that I had come to dread. My knees started shaking and I felt so scared that I went back into my room and shut the door. I lay down on the floor with my hands clenched and my head rocking back and forth uncontrollably. "Please, God," I kept saying over and over again. "Don't let him die. I'll do anything, but please give me another chance . . . Please don't let him die." Why had I acted so terrible while they were gone? Why didn't I study? Why, why, a million whys were repeated in my head.

I listened to the siren of the ambulance until it finally faded away, and then I lay there on the floor staring at the ceiling as the sky turned from black to gray to a dull white. There was still no sunlight when I ventured out of my room to see if Dorothy or Sonny was up.

Sonny was lying spread-eagled on the tile floor in the

kitchen playing with Pippin. He looked up at me. "Carrie, did Daddy go away because I was bad at dinner?"

"No, of course not," I answered. "You weren't any worse than usual, anyway."

"Will he come back soon?" Sonny asked.

"I don't know," I said, looking over at Dorothy for help. She avoided my eyes.

"Doesn't he want to be home with us?" Sonny went on, grabbing Pippin, who was squirming to get loose.

"Sonny," Dorothy said, "your father is sick. He would be here with you if he could. Now eat your breakfast."

"I don't want this junk," he said, standing up and pushing his plate of scrambled eggs toward the edge of the table.

I stopped the plate just as it was about to tip over.

"Now watch what you're doing," Dorothy cried. "I made those eggs especially for you."

"They look like vomit," declared the Brat, curling his lip at her.

"He's just being obstinate," I told Dorothy. "Ignore him."

"You both hate me," Sonny shrieked. He kicked the table and charged out of the room.

I wanted to go after him, but I knew he wouldn't listen to me. What could I say to him? If I promised him everything was fine, I would be lying.

"I don't know how to handle all this," Dorothy grumbled, banging the pans around. "If it weren't for your dear father, I would be long gone."

"You're doing a great job," I told her. "Sonny gets persnickety, that's all. Don't go leaving us now. We need you."

"That's what your mother keeps telling me."

"Dad's going to be all right, isn't he?" I asked. "Can't the doctors give him some more medicine?"

"I can't answer that," Dorothy replied, dumping the eggs in the sink and wiping her hands on the dish towel. "I just keep praying."

"What good are prayers?" I said crossly. "Nobody's listening."

XVIII

The next few weeks were a nightmare of hushed voices and blurred images of relatives coming and going. A deadly calm settled over the household, except that the phone rang constantly. Dorothy would say, "No, we don't know anything yet." Mother was at the hospital day and night. Every day I would ask, "Is he better? Is he better?" I stayed in my room trying to read, to write stories in my diary, to do anything that would block out the feelings of dread. Nothing worked.

I wandered into the kitchen, where Dorothy was cooking. "It looks like you're expecting an army for dinner," I said. She had made three apple pies, four casseroles of chicken tetrazzini, and five batches of chocolate-chip cookies. Sonny was following her around, dropping cookie crumbs all over the floor.

"Go outside and play," she told him. "You're getting to be what Aunt Miriam calls a nudge."

"You're mean," he said. "Nobody wants to do anything around here any more."

"Come here," I said. "I'll tell you a story."

"Just don't use any big words," said Sonny. "You're always trying to show off."

"Do you want to hear a story or not?" I asked.

"All right, all right," he said. We sat down outside.

"Once upon a time there was a witch named Martha, who lived in a house on chicken legs," I began.

"What did she look like?" asked Sonny.

"Kind of like Mrs. Llewelyn Wasserman," I told him.

"Oh, a mean, fat witch," said Sonny.

"She had a brother named Sam who was always causing trouble—a real nuisance. He reminds me of someone else I know." Sonny perked up. He identifies with characters like that.

"What did Sam do?"

"Well, Sam was clever. He could always think of ways to trick Martha—like hiding her magic broom, short-sheeting her bed, or jumping out and scaring her at unexpected moments."

"I like this story," said Sonny. He smiled an imp's smile.

"So one day Martha decided that it was time to give Sam a taste of his own medicine."

"Oh, no!" said Sonny.

"She knew Sam liked chocolate-chip cookies. She whipped up a batch but added a special ingredient, a secret potion."

"What did it do?" asked Sonny.

"Hold on and I'll tell you," I said, moving closer to him and whispering in his ear. "She put the plate on the table, told Sam not to eat the cookies, and retired to her chambers. Sam sneaked up and stuffed a fistful of cookies in his mouth. All of a sudden, he started laughing, and he couldn't stop." With that, I pounced on Sonny and started tickling him. He squeezed out of my grasp with a yelp and ran down the driveway.

I galloped after him, shouting, "I'm going to get you." We chased each other around the block until we were worn out. Sonny dragged himself inside, turned on the television, and fell asleep.

"Thanks," said Dorothy. "That will keep him quiet for a few hours."

"Well, we both needed to let off steam," I said.

I called my Aunt Miriam and began badgering her. "I have to know what is happening," I told her. "I'll talk to your mother" was all she would say. I kept thinking that if I showed God that I really cared, He would somehow make Dad better.

How could I have been so selfish while they were away? I made bargains and promises. I made lists. I scribbled in my diary.

"Dear Diary," I began, "I promise to stop teasing Sonny even when he calls me Frizzy Head—no, that's dumb, and not important enough." I started over.

"Dear Diary, I promise to listen to Sonny and only call him Brat when it's absolutely necessary. [Advice to bargainers: Never make promises you can't keep.] I won't get so impatient and angry with people all the time. I'll do my homework even when it's as boring as cleaning my room, which, by the way, I'll start doing. I wonder if God has a sense of humor? My dad does, and we need more people like him in the world. I promise to spend every Saturday doing volunteer work at Children's Hospital instead of watching old movies at the Shady Oak Theater. Why is it so hard to be a better person? I'm not sure yet what kind of person I want to be or even who to model myself after. But I promise not to worry so much about being popular or complain about being too tall. I'll even try not to drop so many big words."

When Mother got home from the hospital, I begged her to let me go to see Dad.

Aunt Miriam said, "Elizabeth, I think the children

ought to go visit him, if only for a few minutes." Mother finally agreed. Sonny didn't seem to know what was happening. I had hardly been aware of his existence lately, or anyone else's, for that matter. By now it was summer vacation, so I didn't have to be in school, and whenever anyone called, I told Dorothy to tell them I was not home. When she refused to do it once when Fern called, I screamed at her until she finally gave in and hung up. If Fern heard me in the background, I didn't care.

Jewish Hospital is one of those forbidding institutions that take up one square block of the city. I had never been inside a hospital before. I could feel my stomach muscles tighten as we walked up the front steps and through the wide glass swinging door. The lobby was filled with white-uniformed nurses, several patients in wheelchairs, and visitors lined up by the elevator or sitting on orange-upholstered couches. The place was so modern and plush it reminded me of a hotel, except for the people in bathrobes, who seemed to be moving in slow motion.

Mother pointed out the gift shop and the flower cart, which she initiated with Aunt Miriam during their volunteer days.

Sonny was fascinated by all the activity. His cheerfulness was getting on my nerves, and I told him to shut up and stop asking so many questions. Mother put her arm around him protectively. When we stepped into the elevator, I wanted to turn around and walk right out. I hated being there and I hated my mother and brother for pretending, for being so casual.

The nurse ushered us into Dad's room. "What fine-looking children, Mr. Singer. Now, don't you wear yourself out." She cranked up the bed so that he was in a sitting position. Dad gave her a weak smile. She began collecting empty cups and straightening up the room. I knew he didn't want her fussing over him. Dad's like me in that sometimes he needs to be left alone. And now there was this jabbering lady around all the time. I couldn't wait until she finally scurried out. Yet it was hard to look over at him.

His face was ashen and he had lost even more weight. There were gray circles under his eyes and lines on his face. There were tubes hooked up to him and a lot of strange machinery all over. I felt like a piece of wood as I approached the bed.

"Don't be scared, Carrie," he said to me. His eyes were filled with tears, and I could feel the tears starting to roll down my cheeks. Sonny stood there fidgeting next to the door. "I didn't want you children to see me like this," said Dad. "But I missed you."

"Me, too," I mumbled, swallowing hard.

"Carrie," Dad whispered, pulling me closer, "take good care of things at home."

I don't remember much of what happened next, but I

wasn't crying when we got into the car. I was just relieved that it was over. Sonny was very quiet. He looked so small and helpless, curled up in the back seat. I felt sorry for him, but I didn't know what to say.

"You can cry if you want," I told him, reaching for his hand.

He shrank away from me. "I don't want to cry," he said, scrunching himself up into a ball in the corner.

That night, when everyone had gone to bed, I lay on the floor again in my room. I began my litany. "Please God, please God," I whispered over and over again. I don't know how long I lay there. The sharp buzz of the doorbell brought me out of my stupor. I knew why there was someone at the door this late at night, I just knew. Uncle Mike was standing there, of all people. Why did she send him?

He just stood there for a moment and then said quietly, "I'm sorry, Carrie."

"I knew it! I knew it!" I screamed at him accusingly and ran upstairs to my room.

XIX

I promised myself I would never go to a funeral again, no matter who else died. I stood there next to my mother, watching, nodding mutely as people came up to "pay their respects." Even the Allens stopped by. Mrs. Llewelyn Wasserman was one of the first to arrive, all decked out in a humongous black hat. "I'm sorry you lost your father," she said.

Sonny looked at me. "Will we ever find him?"

"He's dead," I wanted to say. "He's not ever coming back." But the words wouldn't come.

Dorothy said, "Your father is taking a long rest."

"Well, Sonny," said Mrs. Llewelyn Wasserman, "now

you're the man in the family." Mother glanced at her
briefly. Her look was strained. Sonny looked up at me,
baffled. I felt my fingertips go numb. Finally, when Gert
and Dr. Steiner walked in, I couldn't stand it any more
and I burst into tears. Gert took me out into the hall and I
stood there sniffling.

"I wish I could be like my mother," I sobbed. "She
stands there so composed, so charming to everybody. I
wonder if she even cares."

Gert said firmly, giving me a hug and a handkerchief,
"Dry your eyes, Carrie, and go back in there. She needs
you more than you think." So I went back.

Mrs. Allen was saying to my mother, "Elizabeth, if we
can do anything for you, let us know." Mrs. Allen turned
to me. "Courtney will be over to visit you later." I
couldn't tell her that I really didn't feel like seeing anyone right now.

"Thank you, Emily," Mother told her. "I appreciate
your coming."

I was surprised that they knew each other—that they
really seemed to care. I was lost for a moment in the
warmth of their comforting smiles, their arms reaching
out to hold me to them. Soon they were gone and my
mother's words, "Thank you, I appreciate your coming,"
were repeated over and over again—like a teletype machine, a steady rhythm of the same sentence, the din of it
covering her feelings and mine.

We walked down to the hard wooden bench in the front row. The rabbi stood. Mother sat. I sat. Everyone sat. The rabbi talked. His eyes darted from face to face like a worried chipmunk's. He began to talk about Dad: "A fine father and husband, a respected member of the community—" and on and on. Who was this person he was talking about? I knew the rabbi didn't even know Dad. I kept glancing up at Mother and looking away.

I'm glad Dad wasn't here to have to listen to this, I found myself thinking. But then I wished he were right here sitting next to me, holding my hand, crying with me at someone else's funeral. I wondered if it would make him feel good to know that he had so many friends. All the people from the factory were here, sitting together behind us.

Dorothy and Aunt Miriam kept heaving long sobs and blowing their noses. Mother sat dry-eyed next to me, not budging an inch until it was all over. I could feel myself moving further and further away from her into a blank, empty space. It seemed like hours until finally I was able to stand up. We got into a huge, black limousine that was to carry us to the cemetery. The driver kept his eyes straight ahead. I looked behind us at the long funeral procession—the cars winding around like a snake with beady headlights for eyes. There were just Aunt Miriam, Dorothy, Mother, and me in the car. Sonny had been

120

escorted home earlier. Mother didn't see the point of his staying for the whole funeral.

Standing under the black canopy at Chapel Hill Memorial Gardens, I felt like I was in a daze, until they lowered the casket into the ground. Then I realized that we would never see Dad again. My mother shuddered. Like sleepwalkers, we moved back to the car. I looked over at her as she sank down in the seat and began staring out the window. I wondered what she was thinking as the limousine crawled past the stone gates at the end of Cemetery Drive.

"We shouldn't have gone to the club for dinner," she finally said, to no one in particular.

"It did him good to get out, Mrs. Singer," Dorothy told her. "Don't blame yourself."

Who is to blame? I thought.

As if she were reading my mind, Aunt Miriam said, "We all loved him very much, but there was nothing that anyone could have done."

Mother turned and looked at me. Reaching for my arm, she started crying—the sounds coming from deep inside. "I need you so much, Carrie," she said. "We have to try to help each other." I could tell now that she had been holding back her tears for a long time. She was drooped over like a wilted rose. For the first time in my life, I felt sorry for my mother.

121

"I know I haven't been much help lately. I want to try. I want to do a lot of things," I managed to blurt out. What could I say to her? She had never acted so defenseless before.

"Carrie, Carrie," she said. "It hasn't been easy. We've both been hiding from each other."

"What can I do?" I asked her.

Mother straightened up and wiped her eyes. "I've decided to go back to work." The car bounced over a bump in the road. I reacted the same way to her announcement.

"Elizabeth, you didn't tell me," Aunt Miriam said.

"I want to try and run the factory myself," she said.

"Instead of selling it?" I cried with surprise.

"Your dad worked hard building up that business, I don't want his efforts wasted. Besides, I'll need to do something now."

For a moment I had been frightened that Mother would fold up and collapse like a house of cards. Now I felt some of the tension lifting. I wanted her to know that I could be strong, too, even though I didn't feel very strong. I sensed that Dad would have been glad that we were trying to carry on.

"Can I work there, too?" I asked. "I can type and file and stuff like that."

"I hope you will," Mother said, brushing my hair off my face. "You have a long summer vacation, and I can use a helper."

"Do you really want me to?"

Mother nodded.

"Well," said Dorothy, "I guess I'll have my hands full taking care of Sonny while you're in Flat River."

"You amaze me, Elizabeth," said Aunt Miriam, shaking her head.

"Martin would have wanted us to do this."

We held on tightly to each other as the car turned slowly into our familiar lane. As we reached the house, I could see four figures sitting on our front lawn. Oh, no, I thought. It was Fern, Courtney, and Dewy. In the middle sat Sonny. They were waiting for me. What could I say to them? How could I stand for my friends to see me in this awful car? Just their knowing where I was coming from made me embarrassed. Why don't they leave me alone? I slipped down as far as I could in the velvet cushion, but when the car jerked to a halt and I had to climb out, their faces were so full of concern, so expectant, that my uneasiness disappeared. Mother, touching my cheek lightly, said, "Carrie, I need to lie down for a while. You stay here with your friends." Then she hugged Sonny and walked inside. Fern stood up. She was wearing shorts and no more braids. She didn't look fat at all.

Glancing at me shyly, she said, "I've missed you."

"Come on, Carrie," Dewy said. "Let's all walk over to Baskin-Robbins."

"Okay," I answered, nodding at Fern and Courtney. When I grabbed Sonny's hand, he squeezed it back. He didn't say anything. He just held on to my hand. We both held on and walked away from the limousine, away from the house, with my friends close behind us.

XX

I didn't realize that even after the funeral was over, people would keep coming over and bringing things. Within three weeks, we received eighty condolence cards, fifteen flower arrangements, twenty homemade cakes, and ten platters from Slatkin's Delicatessen.

"Why doesn't Mr. Slatkin tell people that we're up to our elbows in corn beef and kosher pickles?" I asked Aunt Miriam, who was busy helping Mother write thank-you notes.

"I guess funerals are good for business," she answered, stacking the cards into a neat pile.

"What a thing to say," admonished Mother. "Although I'll admit I've about had it with salami sandwiches."

"Tonight I'll make tetrazzini, Mrs. Singer," said Dorothy, who was collecting pots of wilted gladiolas and carnations.

"That would be nice," said Mother. She stopped writing and stared absently out the window. I knew she was thinking the same thing that I was. Chicken tetrazzini was Dad's favorite dinner. And here we were, sitting around joking about the platters, and he had just died. For days we had been talking about everything else but Dad; yet everyone was thinking about him, missing him just the same.

Mother looked over at me. I was stretched out on the couch, with my legs dangling over the side.

"Carrie, sit up straight. Don't you have any notes to write?"

"Only about two dozen," I replied. I must have heard from every girl in my class. That amazed me. I wondered how they found out and if their mothers had put them up to it. I was glad to get the notes, anyway. If nobody had bothered, I would have felt terrible. Yet the letters were strange. "Dear Carrie," they started out, "I'm sorry about your recent loss." "You have my sympathy at this difficult time." No one came right out with the word "died." They used "passed away," or "departed," instead.

I answered back on my yellow stationery that says

"From the desk of Carrie Singer" on top. Dad gave it to me for my birthday last year. "Thank you for thinking of me. See you soon. Love, Carrie." The hard part was looking up the addresses, because I couldn't find my Miss Elliot's Buzz Book. Pulling myself up from the couch, I began scrounging around for it.

Mother said crossly, "If you would put your things away, you wouldn't always be looking for them."

"Well, I'm developing my research skills," I told her.

"How about developing your leg muscles and mailing these letters."

"While you're at it, pick up some mushrooms for me at the grocery store," called Dorothy from the kitchen. I could smell the chicken boiling.

Sonny wandered into the room and flopped down next to Mother. He's hardly left her side for a minute since Dad died. He even crawls into bed with her every night. I don't know how long she's going to let him get away with that, but I think it's unhealthy.

"Come to the store with me," I said to him.

"Can I buy a Snickers bar?" he asked Mother.

"Certainly, my lamb," she said, kissing him on the cheek. He keeps asking her how she feels, and he's discovered convenient excuses to stay home from day camp.

"Maybe I better stay here," mumbled Sonny. "I've got things to do."

"What do you have to do," I asked impatiently, "besides sitting around doing nothing?"

"Leave him alone," said Mother. "He doesn't have to go."

"Well, it's dumb to let the Brat have his way all the time," I said.

"Oh, go with your sister," said Aunt Miriam. "Here's a dollar. Buy a special treat."

"Hey, all right," said Sonny, more enthusiastically. He jumped up and grabbed the money.

"Oh boy," I grumbled, "all it takes is a little bribery." I was getting sick and tired of everyone fussing over Sonny. What about me? My brave front was beginning to crumble.

As I picked up the envelopes, I must have given everyone a dirty look, because Mother said in her even, controlled way, "I know you're upset, Carrie. You think I'm not handling things well."

"All you ever do is worry about Sonny," I said huffily. I hate when she talks to me in her guidance counselor's tone.

"Carrie, I don't know all the right answers, either. I'm trying." Her voice faltered. "That's all I can do." When she turned away, her shoulders were shaking. Was she crying over Dad, or was she upset for herself?

Aunt Miriam sprang up. "Carrie, I'm surprised at you!"

"I'm not," I spat back at her. My only surprise was that Mother was actually upset over something I had said, which made me feel worse, not better. I wanted to tell her that, but instead, I walked out. If the Brat wanted to come along, it was up to him to follow.

He did, waving his newly acquired dollar in my face. "I'll share some of it with you, Carrie." He sure knew how to make me feel guilty.

He bounced along next to me, making monkey faces and odd noises all the way to the market. At the checkout counter, I saw Dewy and Scott Carouthers. (Courtney told me his parents threatened to send him to military school if he didn't stop following her around.) Dewy stopped by to see me last week, but there was so much commotion with our relatives eating, crying, and carrying on that I felt funny about inviting him in. Would he have understood that moaning while chomping on kosher pickles was the way my aunts and uncles expressed grief? Today he looked at me in a strange way; so I said "Hi" and quickly ducked down the vegetable aisle.

Sonny decided to buy a hundred sticks of bubble gum for a penny a piece. It took him ten minutes to stuff it all in a bag, and then the checker insisted on dumping the gum out on the counter to recount. I stood there shuffling my feet, looking disgusted. I hoped I would run into Dewy again.

"One hundred and two," the girl announced triumphantly.

"Here, sonny," said the woman behind us, "take these two extra pennies."

Sonny eyed her suspiciously. "How do you know my name?" But he accepted the money. I decided not to butt in, the lady looked so pleased with herself.

"Thank you," he said, giving her his most angelic smile. He could be a charmer, all right.

The lady beamed and patted him on the head. "What an adorable little fellow. I'll bet your mommy and daddy are proud of you," she said.

"I don't have a daddy any more," he said, popping a huge bubble.

"Oh, dear," she said, "I'm sorry to hear that."

"He's dead," said Sonny, without a hint of remorse in his voice. I grabbed his sleeve, headed for the exit, and shoved him through the revolving doors. I couldn't believe how unconcerned he was acting, as if nothing was bothering him. But then he was staring at me—wide-eyed, mournfully.

"Will Dad ever come back to life?" asked Sonny as we started to cross Clayton Road. I was so startled by his question that I didn't notice the light change from green to red. The cars began honking and we had to run all the way across. How could I answer him?

"No, he's not ever coming back." At last I said it out

loud. The words sounded so final. I didn't want to believe them, either.

"Maybe the rabbi and Dr. Herman are wrong. Maybe Dad's not really dead," said my brother.

"I wish that were true," I told him, "but that's impossible."

"Isn't there anything left of Dad?" he said quietly. "Not even a shadow?"

Oh, it's not fair, I thought, clenching my fist. What could I tell him that would make any sense?

"What's left is what we remember, all the good times, all the wonderful things he did with us," I said, hugging him.

"He promised to take me to a baseball game this summer," said Sonny. Now I realized that, to my brother, Dad's not being here was like a broken promise—a broken promise that no one could explain to him. I gulped and rubbed my eyes.

"If I cry," said Sonny, "everyone will laugh and call me a sissy."

"No, they won't," I said. "You can cry all you want. We'll go home and cry together."

"But Uncle Mike told me to take care of Mother and act grown up."

"Uncle Mike doesn't know what he's talking about," I said. "We're all going to take care of each other, and that means crying together if that will make a difference." I was mad, really mad. I stormed into the house and confronted Mother.

"Do you know all the stupid things people have been telling Sonny? No wonder the Brat's confused, with those fools telling him to act grown up and not to cry." Oh, how I missed Dad. How I wanted him here right now. I felt so helpless that I wanted to throw the grocery bag across the room.

"Calm down, Carrie," said Mother. "We'd better go upstairs and talk this out."

"I don't feel like talking right now," I said. "I'm too upset." I went up to my room and turned the stereo on. I needed the music to wash away my anger like waves. I threw myself down on the bed and landed so hard that the bed frame cracked on one side and made a loud, thumping noise. I refused to go downstairs for dinner, but later, when everyone was in bed, I sneaked into the icebox and finished off the leftover tetrazzini. Climbing back into bed, I pulled the sheet over my head like I used to do when I was little. I tried to imagine what it would be like to be dead. I pretended to float, that I was suspended in air. For a while I felt peaceful and quiet, but I began to get nervous. Every time I closed my eyes, my eyeballs seemed to turn around in their sockets as if I were staring back deep inside my head. It was like looking into a black, bottomless hole.

Maybe if I prayed, Dad would somehow hear me. But

when I started the prayer that I've been whispering into the dark every night since I was three, I choked on the words. Then I realized that I hadn't prayed since the night Dad died.

"Now I lay me down to sleep," I mouthed to myself, "I pray the Lord my soul to keep." But when I reached the line "If I should die before I wake," I knew that I could never utter that prayer again. It was hard to fall asleep after that.

XXI

I woke up early the next morning. My alarm clock said
7:30. I wanted to get out of the house, to run away from
the anger that a restless night hadn't cured. I couldn't
stand another day of sitting around writing notes or listening to my mother's friends trying to cheer her up.
Feeling grouchy and tired, I pulled my bike out of the
garage. I might as well ride over to Fern's house. Everyone would be up because her brother, Joshua, is one of
those overactive kids who ramble around the house at
dawn. The problem was riding my bike to Waterman
Avenue through the park alone. I'd never done that before, because Mother thinks it's too dangerous. Well, I'm

thirteen, almost fourteen. I can certainly visit a friend without asking permission, I told myself. But my stomach was jumpy just thinking about it. Imagining wading in the forbidden creek at Miss Elliot's gives me the same kind of creepy sensation.

It was Sunday; the streets were empty and the air was fresh and cool. Pedaling as fast as I could, I kept the gears on the hardest notch to climb the hills, and then I coasted down Clayton Road, with the wind blowing in my face. I didn't put the brakes on once. What had I been so cautious about? This was exhilarating!

But when I reached Forest Park, I began to feel uneasy. There were always stories in the newspapers about bike grabbers and muggers. No one could want this old ten-speed, I thought, looking down at the rusted fenders. It had belonged to Ilene until she turned sixteen. She decided that she was too old to ride a bike any more, so Aunt Miriam gave it to me.

The bike path runs the length of the park. It's straight and smooth and goes directly down Lindell Boulevard to Fern's street. There's one curvy section surrounded by towering old oak trees. That's the only sheltered area on the whole trail. There was no one on the path, not even a jogger. I approached the enclosed part very cautiously. I hoped no one was hiding in the bushes, as I glanced around to see if anybody was following me. A man darted out from behind a chestnut tree. He was wearing a

T-shirt that said "Kiss Me. Nothing Makes Me Sick!" Oh, no, I thought, a pervert. He grinned and passed right by me.

This is stupid, I told myself. You started this. You're almost there. Don't chicken out now. I whizzed right around the curve. The trees formed an arc over my head. A cool, green tunnel. Soon I was out in the sunlight again. Whew! No problem.

Up ahead at the corner, I saw about five boys sitting on the curb. They were laughing and smoking. They looked up when they saw me coming. Maybe now was the time to turn around. One of them started to run toward me with his arms outstretched to block my path. His hair was like straw. As if a scarecrow had suddenly come to life, he flopped toward me. He was gesturing wildly, a beer can in his hand. I was petrified. What do I do now? He kept running faster and faster. Just as he reached me, I swerved my bicycle onto the grass and tumbled over.

When I pulled myself up and jumped back on the bike, the boys hooted and jeered. My knee was scraped and I felt a dull throbbing in my shoulder. But I was so angry that I could hardly feel the pain. I wasn't scared any more, just furious at those dumb jerks. They pointed and shouted at me, "Hey, what's the matter? Where are you going?"

Before I got to the corner, I rode into the street and

screamed back, "You're a bunch of imbeciles! You ought to be locked up!" I had never yelled so loudly. My voice sounded like thunder in my ears.

The boys stopped jeering and backed off. I felt a sudden sense of freedom. I don't know how I went from there to Fern's house. Maybe the bicycle grew wings; maybe it was whisked up by the wind and dropped on her doorstep. All I knew was that I had made it—right through the tunnel, right through those stupid boys. Even if I'm in trouble, I thought, nothing can take away this new feeling. Only after I got off my bike was I aware of my body again.

I staggered up the walk and rang Fern's doorbell. Gert had installed a contraption so that when you pressed the buzzer a chime rang out the first four notes of Beethoven's Fifth Symphony. Ta-ta-ta-tummmmm. The dogs scrambled around inside, howling ferociously. No wonder they'd never been robbed.

"Hold on. Hold on." Gert's voice boomed over the intercom. "Who's there?"

"It's me—Carrie," I shouted back. How could she hear me over all that racket?

"Takes all my strength to hold on to these beasts," said Gert when the door was finally opened. "Hey, what happened to you? Your leg is bleeding. Come inside and tell us what's the matter."

Then I was laughing and crying all at once, repeating

the story of my narrow escape. Soon Joshua, Fern, Gert, and even Dr. Steiner were gathered around me.

"Well, well," said Dr. Steiner, "you've had quite a time. Does your mother know that you bicycled here all alone?" All of a sudden they were quiet, looking at me.

"No," I muttered, looking down at the floor, "but I, I . . ."

"Don't worry about it," interjected Gert. "I'll phone Elizabeth right away and tell her Carrie's here safe and sound."

"You'd better come upstairs and clean up," said Fern. "Gosh, Carrie," she declared when we were alone, locked in her bathroom, "that's what I call an adventure." Fern never says ordinary things like "You shouldn't have done that," or "What a stupid idea." "Now," she said, "tell me the motive."

"I'm not sure, except that I needed to get away from the house for a while."

"I guess you're having a rough time," she said sympathetically. I nodded, feeling my eyes fill up again, biting my lip.

I splashed cold water on my face and bandaged my knee. I rolled my shoulder around. It was all right, except for being stiff.

"My mother's going to be upset," I said. "I don't care. I'm not going home." My voice sounded low and hoarse.

"Girls, may I come in?" called Gert at the door.

"She always wants to get in on everything," complained Fern, unlocking the door.

"Your mother said she'll be over to pick you up in an hour."

"Can't I stay here?" I asked Gert. "I'm going crazy at home."

Gert pulled on her bangs and eyed me critically. "I would love to have you here, Carrie. You know that." She paused. "Did I ever tell you that my father died before I was even born?"

I shook my head. All I knew was that she grew up in Brooklyn, near my grandparents' store.

"Did he get sick, too?" I asked.

"No, he died because people around him were sick," she answered. She began telling me all about how her mother met her father in a pastry shop in Munich, Germany. They split the last apple strudel and it was love at first sight.

"My father's parents, who were very rich, didn't approve of the match, because my mother was an uneducated peasant, a farm girl from Bavaria."

"No wonder you don't like snobs," I said.

"They were married anyway," Gert continued. "My father was studying law at the university around the time that Hitler came into power. The Jewish students were forming groups to protest. One evening a fight broke out with some Nazi supporters. My father was shot. A week

139

later he died. Before he was even buried, my mother fled to the United States to live with her cousins in Brooklyn."

"What happened to your dad's family?" I asked.

"They all died in the concentration camps."

"Show Carrie the pictures," said Fern.

We went into the Steiners' bedroom and out from under a pile of magazines Gert produced a faded photograph of her parents. They were so beautiful, framed in their innocent world. A tall, distinguished man smiled into the eyes of a rosy-cheeked woman, who reminded me of Gert.

"I'm still angry about what happened to my father," said Gert. "So I can understand how you must be feeling right now, Carrie. Maybe your mother and Sonny feel that way, too."

"I don't understand why Dad had to die," I blurted out. "I'm never going to—I don't understand what went on in Germany. Why does God let those things happen?"

"A lot of sad things happen," said Gert. "*Why* is a hard question to answer."

As I peered at the photograph, I thought about the way Dad used to smile at Mother. I realized how much she must be missing him, too.

Then the doorbell was ringing, ta-ta-ta-tummmmm; the dogs were barking; and Mother was calling up the stairs, "Carrie, are you ready to go?"

"Thanks, Gert," I said, giving her a big hug. I flew down the stairs and out to the car with Mother.

She didn't say anything. It's the calm before the storm, I thought.

She was wearing a blue pants suit and smelled of Joy perfume. She pulled into a gas station and handed me a bag from the back seat. "Go in the ladies' room and change your clothes. I want you to drive to Flat River with me today and help straighten some things out at the factory before it reopens tomorrow." She gazed at me solemnly, but her brown eyes held love. She wasn't going to yell at me for bicycling through the park alone. I knew she wouldn't later, either. My chest filled up with a strange happiness. All the way to the ladies' room of Sam's Service Station, I kept repeating over and over in my head, "She really does want me to help. She really does."

XXII

For the last three weeks, every Monday, Wednesday, and Friday, I have been making the long drive to and from Flat River with Mother. On Tuesday and Thursday, she meets with clients at Dad's downtown office. On Saturday and Sunday, she jogs, has a tennis lesson, lunches with Aunt Miriam, or has her hair done at Mr. Jon's Beauty Salon. Aunt Miriam says that Mother's pushing herself too hard. If you ask me, Mother is keeping herself busy so she won't have to think about Dad.

Every night after dinner, she and Sonny sit down and read a story together. Then they have a discussion. I'm supposed to listen, too. The first book was about a little girl who finds a dead bird and buries it. The best line is: "And every day until she forgot, she went and sang to her dead bird and put fresh flowers on his grave." The second book was about a boy whose grandfather dies. The last line is: "He won't forget his granddad, but now it's time to play." Sonny's favorite story is about a little boy named Bernie. When Bernie's dog dies, he tries to write ten good things to say at the funeral. He can only think of nine, until he begins to help his father in the garden. Then he decides that the tenth good thing is helping new plants grow. I think the books are worthwhile because Sonny's not sleeping in Mother's bed any more and he's decided to plant a garden. He dug a flower bed right in the middle of the front lawn. This time I was glad Mother let him have his way.

I've been keeping busy, too, working at the factory. People are nice to me there, especially the secretary, Miss Pettybone, who's been teaching me to file. Sometimes I bet I annoy her, because I ask so many questions. But Mother tells me I'll never learn unless I ask. Miss Pettybone, tiny and always darting around like a nervous rabbit, assigns me a different task each week.

First I sent letters to all Dad's clients assuring them that "the fall production will arrive as scheduled." Then I learned how to operate the stitching machine. The women in the machine room were friendly and laughed and told each other jokes all day. Sometimes they teased me and asked if I had a boyfriend yet. "With those eye-lashes," said Lucy, the pattern cutter, "it won't be long." I pretended to look mysterious, raised my left eyebrow, and shrugged my shoulders.

The problem with working on the stitching machine was that I had to sit bent over for hours. The needle darted in and out of the leather holes. My eyes started itching. One slip and the pattern was ruined. Twice in one day, I almost caught my finger in the machine. Every once in a while, one of the other girls would yell out a cuss word, so I knew I wasn't the only one. I was always glad when the bell rang at five o'clock.

Late one afternoon, as we dragged ourselves out to the car, Mother said, "Carrie, you're doing a great job. Pretty soon you can take over and let me become a lady of leisure."

"That will be the day," I told her. "You love working at the factory."

"I guess you're right, Carrie. It's a special place."

I knew she meant special because of Dad. I feel the same way. Working at the factory, Mother and I are close to Dad in a funny way, and closer to each other, too.

As I leaned my head against the seat, I thought about my mother, the executive. I can tell everyone at the factory likes her, but they don't know what to make of her yet. Mother, with her exotic tastes, has come up with a new shoe style—loafers made in every color of the rainbow. People at the factory are all buzzing about it. She says it's boring to wear brown loafers all the time, so she's decided to manufacture a new line called Razzle-Dazzles. Her advertising slogan is "Stride with Pride in New Razzle-Dazzles." They come in an assortment of colors: peacock blue, magenta, emerald, apricot, and terra-cotta (a fancy name for brown). She looked up the names in my thesaurus.

"Just think, Carrie," she said with eager anticipation as we were speeding down the highway, "you'll have a different color pair of loafers to wear every day when school starts next month." I loved these rides home. Mother and I talk and laugh a lot. Occasionally, I even give her advice.

"Mother," I said, "I hope that somewhere in the United States people will be wearing Razzle-Dazzles this fall, but it's definitely not going to be at Miss Elliot's Academy. That place is the last bastion of conservative America."

She looked disappointed. I didn't want to put a damper on her enthusiasm, but I had no intention of wearing multi-colored loafers to school. I was jittery enough at the prospect of going back. The thought of showing up in magenta shoes did not put my mind at ease. But Mother has already received two hundred orders. I hope Razzle-Dazzles are a big success.

When we pulled into the driveway, Sonny was digging up the zoysia grass. I ran inside to answer the phone. Courtney was whispering in her most confidential "I know something that you don't know" voice: "I have a fantastic goodie for you."

"Oh, really?" I said, acting indifferent. I knew she was dying to tell me.

"Guess who wants to take us on a picnic?" Now I was really curious.

"Let's see," I answered. "Robert Redford, or Mr. Beardsley?"

"Scott called and said that he and Dewy want to explore the woods behind Oak Knoll Park tomorrow. They wanted me to call and invite you to go, too. I'm definitely going, and Mother said she'll fix a picnic lunch."

I guess Scott Carouthers is still following Courtney around.

"Why doesn't Dewy call and ask me himself?" I said. I was so excited that I could hardly hold on to the phone.

"He wasn't sure you would want to, with your father —with—well—uh, you know. He just felt shy, I guess. But please come, Carrie. Mother says I can't go unless you do. She figures I can't get in any trouble with you along."

"Thanks a lot," I said. "Hold on, I'll ask." Mother agreed immediately. She even looked pleased about the

146

whole idea. Maybe her daughter wasn't going to be a wallflower after all.

"Be ready at ten o'clock. Scott and I will be over to pick you up on our bikes," Courtney ordered and hung up. She never bothers to say goodbye. I'll bet she organized the whole thing.

The next morning around nine-thirty I began checking the street. I peeked through the crack in the living-room drapes about every five minutes to see if Dewy was outside yet. I kept fussing with my hair, put lip gloss on, and dabbed musk oil behind my ears. I gobbled down two corn-beef sandwiches for breakfast. Finally Dewy appeared. He began adjusting the gears on his bike. Even though he looked very busy, I caught him glancing over at my house several times.

Strolling outside, I crossed the street and asked casually, "Can I be of service?"

Without looking up, he said, "Hand me the pliers on the ground; my gears are stuck." Pretty soon we were both tugging on the chain, which was jammed between the gears.

"Let's use a stick to force it up," I suggested. Dad had taught me how to fix a bike. "How did you do this?" I inquired. I figured I had a right to know, now that my hands were all covered with grease.

"I shifted the blasted gears too quickly up the hill to Oak Knoll Park."

"You've already been over there?" I asked. A terrible thought flashed through my mind. Maybe he's changed his mind about the picnic.

He glanced at me for the first time, saying bashfully, "Scott and I scouted the place out yesterday to find the best place for a picnic."

I didn't feel so silly any more. In fact, I had an urge to wipe the grease smudge off his nose. Catching my eye as I reached up, he winked. Then he was leaning over, his lips brushing mine. The kiss felt cool and dry. It was over too soon.

From up the block, there was a peal of raucous laughter as Courtney came careening down the street, with Scott close behind. Dewy moved away from me, but we were still looking at each other, sort of surprised, when Courtney wheeled her bike expertly on the grass. "Everyone ready?" she cried. She had on purple short-shorts and a bright red shirt. I was now wearing a secret smile. Huffing and puffing, Scott came lurching toward us, his Day-Glo hair flaming in the sunlight. Attached to his shoulders was a huge pack bulging with surprises.

"I'm not carrying this monster all the way to the park," he complained sullenly. "What did your mother stick in here anyway—rocks!"

Courtney is good-natured about almost everything except disparaging remarks concerning her family. "Just watch out, Scott Carouthers," she said, frowning. "Mother spent a whole hour this morning fixing lunch for us." I could tell she was outraged. Her face turned canned-salmon pink.

I peeked into the backpack. There were individual bags tied with blue ribbons, and a package of paper doilies. I smelled ripe pears and freshly baked bread. Maybe Mrs. Allen has the same fantasy I do about the picnic: a long, lazy day romping on the grass, the colors soft pastels, like a French Impressionist painting. Instead, what I was witnessing now looked more like a cartoon.

Courtney and Scott were circling around each other like wary animals. Courtney was a cat ready to pounce. I had a sudden impulse to stand between them. What if Courtney takes her fried chicken and goes home, I thought. The whole day might be ruined.

"Scott, you carry the food. I'll take the rest," offered Dewy. No wonder I like him. We all smiled with relief. Peace was restored.

"Let's go," Courtney said, her old cheerful self again.

Our bicycle wheels crunched and crackled through the pile of brown leaves scattered on the streets. Even though it was a hot, late-August day, the trees were preparing for winter. The radio blared a tune by the Byrds from its hiding place in Dewy's knapsack:

149

To everything (turn, turn, turn)
There is a season (turn, turn, turn)
And a time for every purpose under heaven.
A time to be born, a time to die;
A time to plant, a time to reap;
A time to kill, a time to heal;
A time to laugh, a time to weep.

I looked at the leaves, at the wildflowers wilting in the sun, at the light that cast its shadow. I thought about Dad, about the last time we walked down this street together. The stars were like a thousand candles and the air smelled of jasmine. I remembered what Grandpa Singer once told him: "Death is like the withering of flowers. When a beautiful flower fades and dies, it never grows back again. But we won't forget how special it was."

I looked over at Dewy. He was singing with the radio, his voice clear and full of life.

To everything (turn, turn, turn)
There is a season . . .

Joining his song, I pulled ahead as we raced up the hill to Oak Knoll Park.